A DARK FANTASY ANTI-HERO ROMANCE NOVEL

THE LAST KING

EVIL TASTES GOOD

A.L. SECORD

THE
LAST
KING

EVIL TASTES GOOD

A DARK FANTASY ANTI-HERO ROMANCE NOVEL

WRITTEN BY: A.L. SECORD

DARK FANTASY WEREWOLF MAGIC PUBLISHING

THE LAST KING: EVIL TASTES GOOD
A DARK FANTASY ANTI-HERO ROMANCE NOVEL
Copyright © 2024 by A.L. SECORD

Thank you to my friends and my Sullivan and McEwen family that love and support me. A Big Thank you to: God; My Spirit Guides; Guardian Angels; Trinity and Tori Secord; Andrey Trushin; Bradley Sullivan; Ellen Irvine; David Fox; Shelley Druet; Annie Bishop, and Kent and Megs Garlough. Thank you fans from all of my heart and soul.

DARK FANTASY WEREWOLF MAGIC PUBLISHING Copyright © 2024
This book is available in eBook, and print formats.

Edited by: APRIL SECORD
Book Cover design by: APRIL SECORD

EBOOK ISBN: 9781998151097
PAPERBACK ISBN: 9781998151080
HARDCOVER ISBN: 9781998151103

First Edition: JULY 2024
10 9 8 7 6 5 4 3 2 1

CHAPTER 1

THE FORGOTTEN TOMB

The earth violently shook and cracked the town's peace monument. It was the biggest earthquake since 1669 and split a thirteen mile long fissure through the small town straight into the forest leading to the mountain. The townsfolk paused from their daily routines and then ignorantly went back to their lives; unobservant of the clear path cut to the mountain. They cared not for coincidences and although the three-second quake was fearful; they ignored the simple fact it would lead them to something greater than their mortal lives could fathom.

The townsfolk never went into that part of the forest nor wished to acknowledge it. Not since the great witch hangings and burnings happened. And even now there were too many disappearances surrounding those cursed woods.

The mountains gloom shook and mud slid off the inside of a cave's walls. The rocking had awakened the bats from deep within and a section of cave that had been encased in heavy rock and thick mud. The now exposed entrance breathed as the hot summer wind swirled life into the forgotten tomb.

A set of oozing eyes opened as the mud slid off its festering face. The troll suddenly remembered his mission and broke clear from the wall he had been trapped in. He had a job to finish and it would be easy, as his foe was still embraced in the wall across the room in front of him. His enemy's sword lay before his fungi-filled feet. In this moment the only thought was the medal of honor he would get when he brought the carcass back to hell.

"Ha, the great King Artorik, the last of the knights of Avalon, and the last true King ordained by God; to be slain by your own sword. How fitting and pathetic; what an end. It's nothing personal. But you were raised from the grave to lead the legions of hell. Not serve the light." The troll paused to wipe the snot across his arm and the slime out of his eyes.

"Such a pity but your death will bring me rewards. So this is goodbye oh great King of the Demons; back to hell with you now and forever-more unrest. So I can be the new General." He spoke with such zest as he smiled and grabbed the sword that seemed to slip out of his hands.

Bending down the troll grabbed the sword and dropped it on the first real swing completely missing his trapped target. A loud clang echoed throughout the cave almost sounding like church bells vibrating off the cave walls.

"Excalibur only answers to me." A quiet, distinguished voice came from behind the now trembling troll.

The troll froze and looked in horror at the bright, red glowing eyes now in front of him. And as the last drop of blood was being sucked out of him, the troll thought; *Damn, I really screwed up this time. Hopefully the powers of darkness let me come back again instead of the other traitor.*

"I'm afraid that won't be possible my fellow creature of the night. My truly ugly foe, there will be nothing left of you to return to this world. I plan on devouring every stinking inch of you." The enormous bat-like-creature spoke in his British accent not through malice but of pure, primal hunger as his giant fangs still dripped of the black, sludge-blood.

As the troll's eyes faded out into the void; his parting image was of massive jaws tearing into the flesh part of his forearm. Then the bright phosphorus eyes scanned the half-lit room for their beloved sword.

"Excalibur, you old she-devil; tempting that poor small-brained beast; he didn't have a chance. After all, the lady of the lake did bestow you upon my good graces." The creature smiled warmly as he spoke softly to his sword like that to a lover.

Picking up the sword gently he cleaned off the blade with his family crested handkerchief made of fine silk.

"I am afraid we have slept for too long, and wandered for centuries. The time of the Knights will rise again, but not yet. I can feel the magic here but the evil is not at full capacity. Not yet, anyways." He gently kissed the shining blade that seemed to hum back.

Then he sheathed the sword. He unbuckled the holster from his waist and then raised his hand levitating the sword back to the furthest muddy wall. The sword was suspended in the air hung by some invisible force of magic yielded by his hands and then in a push movement he re-buried the sword back into the wall.

He looked down at the blue dragon on his armor, forged from the steel of the heavens. *What a time of dragons and unicorns; and fighting the evils of the world. Only to become that what I have hunted. Merlin was right the magic that gave me my powers and kingdom changed me as my hatred grew. I am eternally bound by that which I do not serve. Such dreary thoughts to wake up to...Must be the troll's blood.* King Artorik thought as he discarded his armor and chain mail.

Even though centuries of mud had covered the gleam of gold and jewels encrusted in the metal and crown; he could always smell the blood embedded in the glory.

With one wave of his hand he levitated the armor and crown over to the same hiding place as Excalibur. *There; I will bury my lost kingdom from my sight and heart. May that dragon sleep forever.* He thought as in one more wave of his hand, the items were hidden deep within the muddy cave wall.

"I am sorry my old friend. We shall battle. But there will be some time passing through the hourglass of life before the rise of the dark forces. I need to get acquainted with this new world and blend in with the mortals again." He spoke softly to Excalibur that was still hidden behind the wall of mud in the cave.

A melodic voice answered back; "You can never hide the truth of whom and what you are for long, my King. You are still appointed by God; The Oneness. I shall be waiting for you when you need me; King Artorik Dracule Pendragon. You only need to call for me and I shall appear. "

His monstrous wings folded around his body like a cloak as he took a long blue claw to pick out a piece of toe from his fangs. His nine inch fangs were still dripping with the slimy blood of the dark souled troll. Breaking the toe free from his jagged teeth; he crunched happily on the flesh, bone, and nail. *What a decent snack. I must have been a sleep for a very long time. My famine will need at least three more bodies to be reversed and satisfied. I am ever groggy this new dawn of time. I wonder if this will be the age of the great prophesy between the light and dark?* Artorik thought as he looked out into the meadow.

The sun streamed through the opening of the cave as he looked at the shimmering, gold and continued walking towards the light. If anyone happened to be in the forest they would have heard the long horrific groan and seen the monstrous-bat stretch his blue wings and body to the sky. What had seemed like an eternity of slumber had made him stiff and starving.

He stepped into the sun feeling his skin on fire and was contented by the slight smoke he was emitting. Although centuries had gone by and he was too evolved to catch fire like the good old days. *My lovely roar through the forest should have given enough of a warning to the dark magic of the woods that I am waiting for them. And if the sun can't kill me or fire; I sincerely doubt anything else can. The woods seem so alive with life; I hope I can tame myself and not eat everyone.* Changing in the blink of an eye back to his human-form he ran through the field of wild roses and lavender; to the wide river flowing down the mountain.

Charging like a bull he ran into the depths of the cool water to purge the sins from his soul. *Please God forgive me, for I know I shall sin again and again. Forgive me for knowing that love was the only way to defeat the darkness instead of the hatred that consumes me now and forgive me for the undying need to eat the flesh and drink the life-force of the living.* As his thoughts prayed for the souls taken and his soul infused with the light and dark; he opened his mouth to drown out his sorrows.

Even though his lungs had not breathed air in centuries; they held the memory and he started choking. Impossibly drowning in the water through the muscle memory of a lifetime; a nearby creature dove in and bit down hard on his arm dragging him to the shore.

The wolf's white coat shook off the water transforming to a beautiful woman. He could feel her doing compressions and breathed life into his chest; as her long hair dripped over his undead body. His eyes opened into hers filled with the red glow of the damned and she suddenly backed away. He closed his eyes again and gasped for air, sitting up quickly as his brain remembered he didn't need the oxygen to live. Still the muscle memory of his lungs forced his chest to heave in and out.

His eyes went wild and filled with wanderlust; as he saw her bare skin running into the woods and then transform back to the wolf.

He could still feel her warmth as he put his fingers to his mouth to touch where her lips had been. *Thank you my fair lady. A true gem is the fragile creature that can save this horrific, beast. Our paths shall cross again, but as for now...I need to eat. The village is calling me away.*

Staying in the shallows he continued to wash the red clay off his tanned skin. His skin had always had a touch of sun-kissing allure. *Thank goodness for my thousands of days of the crusades and being in the sun. And thank goodness for all of my times as a boy lying by the creek side and playing in and out of the willows; or else my skin would have the pale-blue from being dead.* He smiled at those thoughts and at seeing the yellow eyes along the river and the flash of white fur. She was still there and he heard her heart racing as she silently watched him bathing. *In the olden days it was a life for a life. But I wonder if it still counts with my old foolish-mortal memories? I wonder if she now knows that I am of the undead variety?* He smiled with his fangs elongating as his red eyes met her soft yellow wells; and then his eyes changed to his Kingly, soft gray-blue.

Anyone who truly gazed into the depths could see the centuries of wisdom; if he chose to reveal his soul. And today he did. He felt gracious to this supernatural creature that just recently bonded over him. But his stomach growled through the forest, as his hunger took over his mind.

He quickly turned from the white wolf; needing food over cleanliness. His back faced the wolf as he looked onto the direction of the mountain closing his eyes to echo-locate the nearest villager he could steal clothes off and mortals he could possibly eat.

Splashing broke his concentration as the intoxicating smell of blood was at his bare feet. More river noises occurred as he opened his eyes to a dead buck; which instantly made him praise heaven; and the beast in him took over; tearing into the fur and ripping tendons. *God am I famished. Thank you Lord for giving me substance and for letting me not eat the poor villagers.*

As he started to suck the eyeballs out of the skull, he looked over to the wolf still watching but eating their own ferret, as well. It was a strange sight as the two creatures devoured their feasts together but across the river from each other. If it had been a scare contest though; the giant, vampiric-bat crunching the skull and slurping the brain; clearly would have won. As even the wolf whimpered at the sight and ran off into the forest. *My beautiful, fellow dark creature; I have no etiquette for my hunger right now. I will catch up with you later, but for now I need clothes and to fit in with the mortals.* The King finished devouring every inch of the buck and then went back to the river. Changing back to his old human-form; he changed the waters to a deep crimson in getting the remnants of his snack off his skin.

Then he stood in the long grass and ferns on the dewy river bank. Sniffing the air he could smell the direction of where the she-wolf was heading but it was away from the village. And he needed to find out what year this was and even where he was. *I remember travelling far from my Kingdom in Avalon, even crossing oceans. I remember the crusades and hunting the evils of the world.* He paused to reflect on events long ago and tried to remember the last time he heard his own heartbeat. *I remember the witches being trapped in the woods of Avalon.*

I can't remember why though, they were such a flowery-apothecary bunch of healers; and it was a soft beautiful kind of magic....Ah yes...healing me...bringing me back from the dead to vanquish the evil that was hunting them. It had cursed me and them. But I became more deadly, unnaturally immortal. I became the monster of all monsters. If it weren't for all my mortal years of thirty-three; I would have become the ruler of the world and feasted on even them. He stopped and closed his eyes once more basking in the sun as he stretched his arms to heaven and got on his knees. *I remember there was this small village with huts and the earth had shook. This mountain had encased me and the hell-troll. Excalibur was leading me to where the future war would begin.* He grabbed some soil in one hand and let the loose dirt fall through his fingers; while he echo-located the village far down the mountainside and through the deep woods.

His thoughts stopped on an ancient stone shack smelling of death, far down into the forest before the village. He got up and casually strolled through the forest getting familiar with the woods. He could take his time, as his hunger was subdued for now. For an immortal all life consisted of was an eternity of never ending time.

He stepped inside the broken stone foundation; not needing an invitation as half the building was gone and the roof was missing. He thought about the endless wars against the humans and magical creatures. Even in all his crusades he had never found another immortal such as himself. It was an ironic situation because as the centuries grew; the legends of King Artorik and the knights of Avalon had faded. But the stories of vampiric monsters grew and remained ever more present today than ever before; as he looked at an old pictogram of a giant bat killing a cow on the sides of the stone walls.

He robbed the skeleton of the torn clothes and boots. The worn leather long coat was the perfect disguise of someone who didn't want to be recognized.

A small meow came from around the corner of the wall. The tiny kitten was an orange ball of fur and came running to the only other being it had seen since its first stages of life.

"Awe, aren't you are a sight for sore eyes. This was not the companion I was hoping for dear Lord; but thank you. I think I shall call you Merlin, in dear memory of my old friend. You know he could transform into any animal. Gentle now my little beast, and I shall take care of you." He petted the kitten and then scooped the softness up; putting the little kitten in his inside deep pocket. *Great I'm going to be a lonely old King of the mountain with a cat. Next stop the small village with the little huts. Maybe we can find some food for you and some more food for me.* He smiled at those thoughts and stroked the kitten's soft fur. He walked further down to the edge of the woods and stopped just before the dirt road.

CHAPTER 2

THE VILLAGE BECAME A TOWN

The small woodland village was now much bigger. No more were the huts and cabins of a few; the village had grown to a thriving town. There were dirt roads instead of the dirt paths to the woods. There were wooden and brick buildings of sturdy structures everywhere. There were men practicing medicine; gone were the shamanic women healers. So many little shops had turned up. He could hear the stories being told in the barber shop and in the tavern.

As he strolled through the dirt streets; he listened to the townsfolk conversations of gold and how the bank had been robbed again. He tried to blend in, but he looked like an outsider. He heard people whisper as he passed by the local trade-general store. The townsfolk were a gossipy bunch and did not like hobos. The most common of terms was "Gypsy"; heard as he passed a lady with a long petti-coat. She whispered in such a rude tone his eyes met hers and took her breathe away with his magmatic gray-blue. The animalistic charm he possessed when he looked into others' eyes was purely addictive to mortals. He broke the gaze as the woman's jaw dropped and she stopped locked in his lingering trance. He passed her as she shivered and he went back to looking down and away from the now scandalous eyes that tried to pursue him.

Horses and decorated carriages passed him. Fancy folk with the dignified air of snobbery he had been used to all his palace life.

But the crusades had changed that. The crusades had opened up his eyes to the real sorrows of the world and the starvation of the good people had changed his heart. It was that change that had also transformed him to hunting and hating all the evils of the world; be it beast or mankind.

As he meandered about in the town, he seen more flannel shirts and spiked boots than he had seen since the 17th century, in Wales. *Who would have thought it would be such a woodland statement?* He thought as he watched a group of lumberjacks walk by. The manliness was intoxicating as he wanted to bleed out the testosterone and munch on muscles like ham sandwiches.

As he continued to listen to the town's gossip he found the local *'Acta Diurna'* crumpled up and discarded against a building. He smoothed the pages to read the date of October 30, 1869. *I have been asleep for a century, but even more unfathomable is that I have been undead for over a thousand years.* He thought as he blended in with his flannel shirt and watched the passersby's; continuing to walk along the cobblestone.

Pretty parasols went by with their distinguished arm in arm gentleman escorting ladies to the general-trade store. *The ladies have adopted what I heard is the new empire-waist, and quite fashionable. Little do they know that the Romans wore it first.* He smiled at that thought and watched a group of ladies flock by with their pale silks and bonnets. He smiled as the ladies were much too deep in a conversation to notice that one of the fair maidens had dropped their light shawl. The shawl almost matched his eerily gray eyes as he quickly picked it up for her.

"Pardon me for the intrusion ladies but I believe your acquaintance has dropped this." His smile and bow in greeting had made a carousel of blushes go around the six ladies. The prettiest one with scarlet curls and blue eyes reached her gloved hand to accept the prized item back.

In a hushed tone she quickly said; "Thank you. I apologize for the inconvenience of my better judgement."

"The pleasure is all mine, and not of inconvenience at all." As he said these words he took her hand and kissed her glove in a delicate gesture of introduction as her friends giggled. Taking the silk offered she curtseyed and took back her hand smiling at this chance meeting with a handsome stranger; and scandalously twirling her parasol.

"Molly we have to get going. We shan't be late but again. Please excuse us good sir, in thanks." One of the maidens said as they grabbed Molly's free hand pulling her away from the King and they now hurried as a group further down the streets.

The fine satins, the bonnets and ribbons; invigorated his almost grim spirit; and he could smell the many spices from the local shops. He could even smell the uisce beatha from the nearby alehouse. Though he had never been fond of excess; he missed having a couple of rounds of possets with Merlin. There was nothing quite like it, in all the world to get your heart racing for battle.

The majority of townsfolk were very rude and ignorant to strangers. Every time he passed a mind he read their thoughts and they were an ugly, superficial kind towards him. He just smiled and moved in-between the mortals.

Just then, a much bigger gentleman bumped into him.

"Hey watch it Scamp."

King Artorik looked into his soul for just one tenth of a second; as the big fellow passed. He saw the darkness that the stranger possessed; and he hadn't seen that specific evil since his ravaging days when kingdoms were terrified of even mentioning his name as it had been synonymous with the streamed crimson that ran down his victim's impalement. *Mmm...Afternoon seconds.* He smiled at that thought and turned after the fellow when another tempting scene caught his pleasure.

A whimsical unaccompanied golden-haired lady was across the street looking at him with such peculiarness that he had stopped following the brute and focused upon this oddity of a beauty. No one usually became aware of his hunting prowess unless he wanted to be known. But her yellow parasol twirled and her lovely eyes were definitely fluttering over in his direction in such a way he felt like a main course. *Highly peculiar is this damsel. Have my powers grown so weak that I can merely be summoned like some cattle?* Quite undignified he thought; but kindly smiled her way and slightly bowed the tip of his cap as custom. *It is too soon for this type of pleasurable encounter.* In snapping his fingers he became invisible quite literally in the passing crowds with everyone so pre-occupied with their own dealings no one noticed his vanishing trick.

Even as she looked still towards where he had been, such a huge crowd of people flocked out of the nearest brothel establishment; she had to turn away herself and step away from being encompassed moving with the boisterous crowd.

The flocking of the streets was rhythmic. The steel grease and gases giving a stench only recognizable to strangers that remembered fragrant meadows. *Carriages are still fashionable. I will have to purchase a noble steed once again.* He looked onto the regency dresses and silver lined trousers thinking about the lost past of another world of fashion.

The corsets had been similar but centuries ago the fabric was more luxurious coming from the finest of silks and satins of Romania. He missed the fondness of the peasants and the court adoration. He missed the ladies in waiting and the royalties' he had parted with.

He heard the giant whistle blowing in the distance, and a giant steel monster on metal rails started moving forward. From his vantage point he could see the eagerness of passengers boarding the beast and leaving uninjured; already in anticipation to their adventures. His sharp sense smelt the coal burning as the whistle blew once more and then roared off into the distance.

His attentiveness in studying the marvels of this new world had made him almost miss the confrontation between a fair lady and this brute of a man across the street. The strange man had been quite villainous as he bellowed and twirled his greasy moustache between his thick fingers. His tied bow was an unflattering puce; the kind that matched his ugly attachment to bullying the fair maiden into an unseen place between the buildings.

King Artorik got there just in the moment before a second man had appeared behind some discarded crates. The other man had hit the maiden over the head knocking her unconscious and showing his craven character. As the bushy-mustached man came closer to the lady he started lifting her skirts and the dastardly intentions rolled off his filthy skin like steam. It was too much for the King's thirst just to stand by and watch.

"Excuse me; I don't believe that's the proper recourse for interactions with fair maidens and not at all how to court a fine lady." King Artorik exclaimed as he tapped the undesirable man on the shoulder but a deep growl came from inside his throat.

"Mind your own...aaahhh." The brute had shouted as soon as he turned and saw fangs protruding.

The loud cracking sound and a male's scream could be heard; as King Artorik's grip tightened lifting the big man off the damsel.

"You fellows won't have to worry about my inconvenience for too much longer. I am too ravenous." King Artorik spoke as he threw the one man against the wall and the other man looked on in terror; not able to scream or move as he watching the leather coat being discarded gingerly over the maiden.

The other man grabbed a lead pipe he found and quickly ran to attack; but the metal of the pipe lay mid-air as the six inch nails closed around just as quick. And another hand seemed to wrap around the man's throat as he stopped squirming to breathe.

"I can see your heart is ripe with the evil I find so delectable." King Artorik spoke eloquently as his forked snake-like tongue started to lick the fear dripping off the man's face.

King Artorik's red eyes large and radiant contrasted his now dark-blue skin; as he sank his canines into his prey's carotid artery. *A death I never grow fond of. But I am grateful for this sustaining plague to society. When will the hearts of mankind change to the peace within?* He thought as he drained every inch of the body and then went to the burly man who still lay with his moustache against the stone mortared-wall. *Mmm...I can still taste the Cornish hen in this man's veins.* After drinking the man's death; he hid the bodies in the darkness of the alley. *How ironic these villains are exactly where they were going to lay her. And how is the fair lady?* His thoughts turned to the damsel suddenly.

In his hunger he had almost been careless to not tend to the very fragile creature he was protecting. He changed back to his human form and slipped his jacket and pants back on. He made sure his mouth was clear of any residual indulgence from earlier and made sure Merlin the kitten was still sleeping in his pocket. He gently sat her up and spoke to her with the same gentleness. "Miss, speak I pray you. Please incline that you are well and then I can speak good morrow to you."

He softly tried to tap her on the shoulder to bring her back to the here and now.

"Miss, are you well? Can I fetch a Doctor for you? Miss are you well? You were in an awful spit of trouble when I happen to come around the corner. But those scoundrels will never cross your path again." His eyes held delicateness towards her, as he patted her hand.

Her pretty eyes were now puffy and one slightly swollen as her left cheek also possessed the evidence of the assault. Her appreciation could be seen in her tearful wells, as she slowly spoke looking into his alluring gray-blue eyes.

"I didn't see the truth of the situation until it was too late...they were going to...How on earth did you ever stop such cads? I feel well enough to leave this place evermore. I do not wish to be reminded of any forgotten memory of what happened." Her tears welled and King Artorik took out the handkerchief from which he still held in his front pocket gingerly offering it to her.

"May you please assist me further? I need to get going, my husband will be looking for me. Thank you in kind. My name is Lois Lovecraft." She sweetly said and handed the silk back.

He carefully took the hanky and her hand; lifting her back to her feet.

"My name is Artorik Dracule Pendragon." He bowed to her while still keeping his eyes fixed to hers as she blushed.

"Pendragon are you a fairytale, my good hero?" She tried to smile but still needed his hand's strength to lead her out of the alley.

"Whatever does the lady mean?" He smiled with such passion she lost her breath for only a moment before answering him.

"You must excuse me I am outspoken. But you have the same name as the legend of the great King of Avalon. He was the last true

King ordained by God to rid the evil creatures of the land. It was a fairytale my Father used to read to me each night." Lois said and blushed.

"Purely coincidence; I assure you that I am neither fair nor royal." He smiled while walking her out to the clamorous street. *I might have to use only parts of my name in the future, less be mocked.* He thought for a moment as he steadied her.

"In the future my dear, please accompany only goodness." He said sweetly as she seemed to be cooing.

"Thank you. This is where we shall part but I hope when next we meet; it will be with more amicable company." Lois curtseyed as a gentleman came rushing over to her from across the street.

"Lois where has thou goest without me? It is not proper for a dignified lady such as your breed and stature; to be in town without her accompaniment. What has happened?" The gentleman took her hands in his and then quickly escorted her arm in arm away from the alley.

"Frederik I assure you I am fine, thanks to a gentleman who saved me. Please let us leave the marketplace and go home."

King Artorik looked on listening to their conversation only for a moment and then went back into the shadows. *She had been relieved in fainting from the brutal slap she received from that giant-moustache of a man. Interfering with mortals has gotten me into trouble before. But I could never stand by whilst someone was in need. The pleasure was all mine fair maiden. Now, I just have to wait until nightfall to move the bodies.* He thought as he made himself invisible and hid in the shadows with the pleasant smell of death.

Feeding slightly on entrails he fed the little kitten still on the inside of his coat pocket that had been asleep until recently. The offal was the perfect snack at this moment; for his and the small fluffs hunger.

The old logging town of Trenton was now busier than when he first stumbled into the small village. Now the thriving town bustled to and fro with petticoats, parasols and gentlemen alike. They had fashioned cobblestone streets on the main road by the hanging square. The wood of the gallows was older than the actual town hall and Mayor.

☘☘☘☘

In the dead of the night he flew with the two bodies back to his cave high up in the mountains. After discarding the bodies he went back to the abandoned homestead and took the furniture creature comforts and pots and pans for those days he wanted to feel alive. He had to accommodate the last human memory or else he truly would be dead to the world with only the monster inside him remaining. The demon creature he was needed the last beat of his undead heart for humanity. He needed to be able to show any form of compassion and to make clear judgement calls on the threats of the world and not just his hunger for it.

After he had turned his cave into a slight home; he returned to the bodies. Nothing would be left of the tasty morsels and the brutes by the time he was finished devouring them. Those scoundrels provided the new funds he needed to possibly get back into the fashions of the world. *Since the year of my birth in 700 A.D. and then dying at the old age of thirty-three and being risen from the grave; I care not for the fairytales of mankind or the realities of their savageness. But it turns out time has not forgotten me as I am no more than a child's bedtime story. Why couldn't I have been a tale of forewarning of what happens when you raise the dead? God, I truly miss the kingdom of Avalon. Maybe I shall never find the hope of happiness or perhaps love again? These stone cave walls will be my salvation for now and keep me on my quest. Although I feel that I am needed in this new world; the uncertainty as the day is long will surely consume me if I don't busy myself. Maybe I shall make a nice stew tonight with all the lovely meat I have lying around. I'm sure my new furry friend Merlin will like that.* He thought as he stroked the little kitten's back and wondered even further; *I hope I am not a fool for adopting such a fragile thing of fur. Maybe he will turn into the fiercest of bodyguards.* He got excited at the thought of possibly teaching the small kitten to attack strange guests that might appear on the mountain. But quickly he doused that bit of happiness as he looked at the kitten snoring.

The small kitten rolled onto its back, dead asleep in his hands. The small creature looked like a remnant of the zombie plagues of 1313 by the Mediterranean Sea. *By Saint Augustine's beard; that little beast is snoring loud enough to wake the dead. I won't do it. I can't let him sleep in my coffin with me. He's such an obnoxious little creature of sweetness. He makes me feel ill.* King Artorik thought as he set the tiny creature down on the cold cave floor.

🌾🌾🌾🌾

CHAPTER 3

HUMAN REGRETS

He carefully ascended out of the coffin's vermilion velvet interior; as to not wake the sleeping beast he had been cradling all night. It was still daylight and the sun was setting just as slow as he was maneuvering. Even as he made his way through the cave he could hear the kitten snoring but see the shimmer of sunlight coming through the entrance.

What a beautiful dreary time of day. He thought as he leaned barely on the inside of the mountain wall. He was allowing the warmth of the sun to embrace him as he closed his eyes and basked. He daydreamt of a vision of his old friend but in this new world. When he opened his eyes he could clearly see the old man lifting his robes and dipping his toes in the water; perched like some giant owl on the rock in the middle of the flowing river. The wizard's long pointed hat was the color of cinder and scorched earth; just like his robes that he had dropped accidently soaking the edges.

The wizard's smile on his rough face had been turned down as he rung out the cloth on the rock. But he smiled and waved to the King just like he used to. He always knew when the King was watching him.

Just as the wizard toppled off the rock; the King was in his long underwear splashing in the river with his ghost of a friend. They frolicked and laughed like the good old days. As the King stretched out on the rock on his back; Merlin lay beside him twirling a piece of reed in his teeth and humming a tune of the old days.

"My good friend is this real? Have you come back to visit and guide me on my noble quest?" The King turned on his side to face his old friend who was still there radiant like the pink and purples of the sky.

"Artorik you are my King and friend for eternity. What is real is between us and heaven. As you know The Oneness exists, and so do I. I am not permitted to reveal myself as I do right now. But you can always find me whenever you need me; in here." Merlin the wizard spoke as he pressed his reed into King Artorik's chest. The long wet piece of grass tickled the King.

Then as the summer breeze blew by something startled the nearby crows out of the trees and King Artorik turned to look in that direction. When he turned back to see his friend's long dripping face; only a wisp was left. The smoke evaporated and the King went back to lying on his side; now chewing the reed that had remained on the rock. He felt like the hollowness of his ribcage was being crushed from the inside and shattering his non-beating heart.

Once again he gasped for air filling his lungs and deeply exhaling out the emotions he was cursed with. A blood tear slowly rolled down his cheek. *I remember you my friend. I remember the promise I made to you; to not get involved with the mortals again. But my destiny is too interwoven. I can't justify standing by as the evils of the world are filling mankind's hearts. I know you would agree with me, if you were alive today.* He continued thinking about his dear friend and teacher. *Must be the old human in me that is out of sorts.* He brushed another tear away as he sat up and gazed across the swaying meadow.

The wildflowers moved in the breeze with the tall grass as he sat up letting himself dry off on the warm rock. Gazing at the wild roses and lavender he remembered the day he found out his friend had passed away. He remembered flying as fast as he could in hope that Merlin was not gone. He was hoping that the rumors had not been true. But they were. And even though death had not been the final performance in his timeline; for Merlin the great magician it was. Merlin had simply gone to sleep one day under the shade of a willow and never woke. *A peaceful and deserving rest to my good friend's life.* He thought as one more tear escaped down his noble skin. *It has been centuries since my mortal emotions bested my regal eyes.* He defiantly thought as he became angry and glared over to the happiness of the meadow.

The forest and fields were alive with the gentleness of butterflies, bees and other non-threatening advisories. Slowly he got off the giant rock splashing into the deep of the river. He made his way to the shore; completely regardless of anyone in the woods watching him. Then he climbed the bank only pausing to capture a bit of merriment through the bold daisy that grew by the stone edge of the mountain. He twirled the happy flower taking in the perfumed scent. The fragrance had captured an essence of the sun and had made him smile for a moment as he looked at the white petals delicateness. He slowly walked back to the cave but stood in the entrance facing the swaying tall grass and flowers.

Then something caught his eye moving in the fields gracefully. He could see the lace and ribbons bouncing with the frolicking maiden as she was giggling. She sweetly called out to the King to join her. His jaw opened un-regally and was left ajar as she danced under the setting sun in her royal nightgown. She jumped back and forth in the ballet of the meadow. The gentle winds were blowing her golden curls; and the sunset had made her shine; almost sparkling in the pinks and deep purples of dusk.

He stood there with his motionless bare feet and scantily clad undergarments watching the fair maiden dance further away. Her thin garment was dangerously hinting at her hidden beauties and his hidden desires for his former Queen. She jumped and danced through the meadow tempting him to come hither. He took a couple of steps outside of the cave just to be able to still see her captivating his heart in the fading sunlight.

But he stopped proudly remembering the past of their cruel love that was not meant to be. There was one moment of happiness they had shared before her heart had been stolen by another. He remembered letting her go back then; just like he turned away from this inviting apparition now. His single blood tear turned the white daisy a deep shade of crimson; just before he stomped it with his bare foot. *Love is for the foolish mortals. I am wild and free from such trivialities.* He stubbornly thought as he turned back and watched Lady Guinevere's spirit still dancing in the distance but stopped to blow him a kiss in farewell. *This is the sweetest sorrow of love. This is the kind of adieu that I wish to not partake in again. My mission is the only thing keeping me here.* He thought as he felt the kiss warm his cheek and then watched the ghost still smiling; kindly vanish.

He stood there looking at the fading sunlight chasing the brightness of the flowers away and wiped another blood tear off his cheek. *Am I to be haunted by every spirit that has ever touched my heart either with kind or evil? Next am I to see Lancelot feasting on Guinevere's heart and then trying to slay me, when I challenged that demon?* That memory had haunted his thoughts as he was not in time to save the kind-hearted

Queen. He had gave his blessing as he needed to fight in the crusades; and never thought the evil would be from inside his own walls. Then he was burned alive with his knights; betrayed by the humans he had been fighting for with the rise of the new Pope. *The witches had not known what they were dealing with when they brought me back. I had awakened with all the vengeance of my heart from my life. When they had exhumed me from death they damned my already supernatural soul. I wonder if they knew what was to happen to them and to me?*

He dressed quickly taking care with his new acquired white starched shirt and trousers. Not the scuff he was wearing from before. But he remained using the long leather coat. It may not have been the fashion but he needed to diminish his shine. He was too unearthly handsome to fit in with the average man about town, and his accent and regalness was still with him from childhood and could not be buried no Matter how hard he tried. But he always gained a reputation for nobility as it was in the air surrounding him. He quickly left some small pieces of entrails out for kitten Merlin and left for the thriving town.

❦❦❦❦

He strolled back into flocks of people. He was grateful to be back with the living. Trenton was busier than a hive of bees as he watched and waited in the shadows of the alleyway. *I can smell the goodness and the sins of mankind. I doubt I shall find trouble finding another meal soon. That poor fool will make me complete again.* He smiled at that thought and then frowned as he saw a man purposefully bumping into others scooping his hands into the pockets of long petticoats and surprisingly trousers. The thief was never caught but he had done it multiple times within the last few minutes.

Faster than the speed of light he moved so quickly through the crowd, neither they nor the thief had time to even blink before he apprehended the individual and swept him up to the mountainside but stopped in the haunted woods. He was going to make this quick but did not want the trail to ever lead to his home. He discarded the greedy man deep in the heart of the forest and then just as quickly moved behind a nearby tree.

"Where am I? I know I was in the town. I know I was borrowing from the Mayor's wife. She always leaves her purse wide open when I am around her." The stranger puzzled blurted out scratching his head and paused to look at the pines and maples of the woods.

"Woah, this is the last time I ever drink the good medicine the Doc gave me. I must have stumbled here unaware in my drunkenness." He scratched his forehead and then made a dash back down the little trail.

But he stopped as he heard a deep growl coming from the path he was running towards. The woods were dark in the thickest parts even on the sunniest of days. But this was dusk and only shadow outlines of trees were visible and the outline of both their white pompous shirts.

The only difference was the slight red glowing from King Artorik's eyes. He wasn't going to hide the intense shade that was pouring into them as he scanned the thief's soul. He could see the cold blooded murders of woman and children. This thief had been promoted in the town gang and the violence had escalated through his sweaty skin. He could smell the putrid scent a mile away.

"You are here in the jury of the forest for your theft and murder of the good ladies and children of the town. I am charging you guilty of crimes unimaginable to the innocents you slaughtered." King Artorik stated and then paused as he saw the thief's eyes widen.

"Your punishment will commence in a third second of excruciating pain; from the ripping off of your arm's left appendage. I will slowly devour you inch by inch until there is nothing left of you in this world.

And I assure you the world will not miss such lowly scum such as yourself." King Artorik darkly said as the thief looked bewildered.

King Artorik slowly unbuttoned his long coat and placed it on the soft grass and then started untucking his starched shirt while he looked at the desperate thief trying to think of a way to save his vile carcass.

"Cannibalism is against the law in this town. I may be a thief. But you're talking murder and eating people. The people of this town will find you and hunt you down like the monster you are." The thief's heart started racing as he stammered out the last words.

The King watched the thief looking at him but too afraid to run. Then King Artorik slowly discarded his shirt, while the thief dug around in his pocket for a weapon. It was clear that the thief had no real hand to hand combating skills as he moved the small blade in front of him like a shield.

"You're not going to take me. My gang will miss me and they will come looking. Just you wait. They'll get you, even if you are the boogeyman."

"Boogeyman, me? Do I look like a hob goblin to you? My name is Artorik Pendragon." King Artorik laughed so heartily but the thief started sweating profusely.

The King took off his boots and trousers meticulously folding them and keeping them together. Then he carefully placed them on a nearby rock.

"Really, you are the great King Artorik? You are the famous man from legends and myths of Avalon; and dragon slaying? That is as humorous as it is to laugh. Why are you in your long John's? If this is meant to scare me; I'm not. The gang knows you got Bubba and Oleg. That sweet lady was meant to be shared with us. I don't care who you are; boogeyman or jester; you're dead." The thief said as he charged sticking the blade into King Artorik's back and now bloodied the long undergarments.

"Well that's perfect isn't it? Have you any idea how hard it is to get blood out from these cotton fabrics? Killing you is going to be more fun than I thought." King Artorik turned around and faced the thief while he pulled out the blade.

Transforming in front of the human was more fun than all the things he had experienced in his lifetime up to this point. The villain clutched his chest in pain and then his mortal heart quit.

"Well now. I guess I won't be eating you alive as I hoped; or executing you. Still you will be some savory treats for me and my little Merlin." King Artorik said with a dignified air as he drained the body; and then flew back with it to the cave.

He stopped at the river to clean up before he went back for his clothes, lost in his thoughts of the bandit. *A perfectly good pair of the longest John's ruined. I'm going to have to go by my middle names or else people will not take me serious. Strange though that they should know of a Kingly name but yet greeted in the face of destiny by it; they turn up their own noses or laugh at the real ideology. And furthermore, who in the blazes started naming undergarments after people?*

CHAPTER 4

ENTER DEMON

The sun was setting and the thirst was upon him again. Maybe since he had been enclosed in the cave walls for a century it was going to take even more blood to get him back to homeostasis. Under normal conditions he could go on the blood of one mammal for a month. But since awakening in this century tasting the vile evil blood had become an addiction. He prayed that the thirst would lament but it persisted until he was forced once again to go into town; not even days after his last hunt.

He slunk to the alleyway waiting for thugs and people of a revolting nature to come out because he knew they couldn't hide themselves away. The mortal he was looking for was an addict of horrendous crime; just like he was an addict of malevolent blood. He paused as he was just going to keep following another thief when he heard several screams deafening his supernatural ears in the distance.

The humans on the street just went about their average business but the King could hear about twenty people screaming inside the fortitude of the bank. He could hear the conversation of a madman who had went in to rob the bank and was now having his way with the women inside. Then he heard the tormented cries as he rounded the street corner. He could hear the gutless gasps of the men who were watching instead of fighting this insane villain.

There was something about this particular situation that sped up King Artorik's undead heartbeat. The madman was so wretchedly evil and Artorik could hear the delight in the madman's laughter as he was torturing people. This robbery wasn't about gold it was about carnage. The madman had become deliciously twisted and his blood was the honeypot King Artorik needed.

Artorik was only a few moments away from getting his necessary fix as he transformed and raced closer to the screams and shouts for help that were growing silent as hope was dying. He recklessly turned his evil up a notch and flew through the front doors of the bank. His blood eyes glowing and blazing. His long sharp fangs revealed in a wicked grin. He even extended his beautiful leathery blue wings which had been hidden from humans for centuries.

King Artorik went full demon vampiric bat with the intent to stop the heart of the madman that didn't even know what had grabbed him from behind. King Artorik could feel the madman's heartbeat that a moment before was racing with a sick sexual desire; but now beat feverishly in terror.

As King Artorik's thick claws extended deep into the madman's back he lifted him to the ceiling while the frightened bank's victims looked on. The woman that had been mid-torture looked up with her weakened wet-eyes and King Artorik's heart broke in recognizing the same lady he had seen before and what this maniac had been doing to her.

A furious roar escaped King Artorik's curled gruesome lips as he savagely sank his fangs into the maniac's disgusting sweat-dripped throat. The madman's throat oozed the delicious evilness the King needed to devour. He drained the madman almost to death; and then slowly turned his prey in his claws like a spider that caught a fly. Ever so slowly; he turned the madman around in his claws to face him. King Artorik wanted the madman to know what death looked like, and to be the last horrific thing the madman saw of this beautiful world. King Artorik wanted to see the foul look of terror in the madman's tear streaked eyes. The King took pleasure in giving a twisted grin as he smelt the urination flowing out of the maniac.

"Mortal, you shall pay for your butchery of carnage. Open your eyes wide to your death. You are the most putrid excuse of a human I have come across in this century. You are so pathetic that even in the next realm the demons wait in glee to torture you upon your arrival. Don't worry my foe; no good deed goes unpunished and all of hell can't wait to rip you apart over eternity." King Artorik's deep, animalistic voice gave all the mortals chills upon hearing.

Even though he knew the humans had been watching this horror show and were terrified speechless; he couldn't stop his pleasure in drinking the maniac's intoxicating blood.

🌾🌾🌾

King Artorik could feel the electricity of the room change to the next level of terror as he held the man with one hand while he ripped out his heart that still slightly pumped. Then he took a huge bite eating the red muscle like an apple. The townsfolk stood with silent screams written all over their faces as King Artorik glanced down whilst he ate the pieces of red fluid heart. King Artorik looked at all the tear streaked cheeks and shocked eyes. He never liked to invade mortal's private thoughts but he listened and was astonished that amongst the emotions of fear was relief; and amazement at the dark creature that hovered before them. The poor simple town's folk had never experienced such malice. They also had never seen such darkness that had saved them and it shook their core beliefs on what was good in the world.

King Artorik had listened to the frightened thoughts of everyone in the high ceiling room. The town's young Mayor had been in the crowd of victims in the bank. King Artorik had been studying the crowd as he ate the vile but tasty heart and his eyes followed the Mayor racing over to the lady that was directly below him. The young lady that had been rescued from the madman's clutches; happened to be the Mayor's wife. As King Artorik drank and devoured the heart; the Mayor embraced his wife and covered her shaken body with his coat.

While King Artorik watched them thinking about what he was going to do to these witnesses, he slowly floated down and dropped the heavy body he had been holding with one clawed hand. He turned around from the Mayor and the crowd. He crutched down slowly transforming to his human-form and retracted his wings into his back.

As he stood up naked with his muscular back to them all, he heard gasps and sighs. He carefully grabbed a long leather overcoat that was hung up on the coatrack. Slowly he did up the buttons as he knew he had two choices in this predicament. He was going to either eat them all or compel them to forget he was ever here. But compelling people always left huge holes in memories and humans were a very curious race.

His eyes were still blood lusted with the rage of the toxic monster he had just finished the heart of. But he still turned to face the crowd and an equal amount of gasps and sighs were heard. He slicked down his hair and brushed off the long leather that now concealed his human looking tanned skin. He looked like a handsome man; except the glowing red eyes. He blinked and his eyes went back to gray-blue and he tried to wipe the blood off his face while he cleared his throat.

"My name is King Artorik Dracule Pendragon. You may address me as Pendragon if you dare. I do apologize for not getting here sooner but to get involved in the affairs of mortals is forbidden. I can assure you this madman is dead and I had great pleasure in extinguishing his light. Pray you shall never meet me again good townsfolk because it will be your death." King Artorik said as he turned to drag the body across the floor while he floated towards the door.

As Artorik continued floating he heard scrambling from behind him. He slowly turned to see the Mayor who had been holding his shattered wife; now standing behind him.

"Please wait. My name is Tom Fields. I am the Mayor of Trenton. We owe you an insurmountable amount of gratitude. You have saved us. I can't thank you enough." The man's shaky voice held true as he stood small behind King Artorik.

"I fear in helping you, I might have awakened the darkness surrounding this town. There are more evils in the world than you could possibly imagine mortal. And I am just a traveler passing through the centuries of mankind. Take heed Son of Adam; the ever war between the light and the dark is presently escaping your small haven in the world but it won't be long." His deep charisma left an ominous foreboding that even though the on-lookers couldn't fathom; their souls knew he was speaking the truth.

"And what are you?" Mayor Tom Fields spoke boldly but his voice held a secret tremble in his soul.

"I am an anomaly. I am beyond death. I am your souls warning of the supernatural and what awaits the wicked. At one time I was human. I am the very King from your medieval fairytales in the time of unicorns, vampires, and dragons. My heart is dark but my soul has always stayed true to The Oneness who bequeathed the crown to me. I used to slay the evil monsters in the world. But the monsters in the world have not the insatiable greed mankind does. But still something wicked and darker will unleash the demons of hell; if evil cannot be stopped." King Artorik slowly touched down to the floor as graceful as an angel but his voice held the dark rasp of something sinister as he cleared his throat.

"You ask me what am I? For that I have not an answer. My undead heart is cold and black. Although, if the Omni-Creator of existence commanded my soul to be set ablaze in the vibrant morning rays and end my life; I would gladly bid farewell at their request. I have found myself for centuries basking in the darkness of blood; but I have felt the warmth, and compassion on the side of the light. So I may have been born from the mother of all dragons; but the only one I seek to please is the true being that is embraced by light. The Oneness is the light; and the light is love. The warmth of a sunny day does not compare to the beauty and forgiving natural magic of the light." King Artorik said as he kept his intense eyes on Mayor Fields.

Then he turned slowly and headed towards the door not giving another thought about leaving the humans and taking the body for leftovers.

"Please wait. I know how vast this world can be and all the wonderful things that are in it. But I too have witnessed the darker sides of life. I was given the Mayor-ship from an accident leaving the previous Mayor decapitated. I believe in co-existence and harmony with all creatures and putting differences aside. I am considered a new-age thinker. You have saved us from a great evil King Artorik Dracule Pendragon and I would like to hold a celebration in your honor." Mayor Fields stepped forward and King Artorik turned in hearing his footstep.

The Mayor's voice was still trembling but that little step of courage was enough for King Artorik to divulge in listening to the Mayor for the moment before he compelled them all and erased their knowledge of his existence.

King Artorik stood there as the twenty people in the bank including the Mayor; stood there jaws gaped deeply staring at the otherworldly being. He knew they were all surprised to what they were seeing, and hearing. They were breathless and speechless. This was all unheard of for the superstitious townsfolk.

"Please stay King Artorik Pendragon. Please continue to help my people. I am offering our community as your own and I offer a commission as a Chief in charge; the Sheriff position, for all of eternity until you deem it necessary to leave our small town. I never want what has happened on this night to ever happen again. If there is more evil coming; I fear we will perish as a community. I dread at the thought of what would have continued if you were not here. This man that you have slaughtered has been killing for a long time and torturing his victims beyond recognition. We have been finding bodies for years in our community. I could never have believed that such a human was capable of such atrocities. The pure fact that this monster has come out of hiding to torment a bank full of people has shown his lunacy; and his commitment for relishing in acts of cruelty and pure evilness." Mayor Fields said as he looked disgusted at the lifeless body of the madman.

"Mayor Fields, I am honored but..." As King Artorik started to speak he suddenly stopped.

He sharply turned his head to the lady known as 'Molly' and Mayor Tom Fields' wife. King Artorik's wings extended out and he ripped the back of his new leather jacket; transforming quickly. He walked over to Molly and past the shocked Mayor that had just gasped. His eyes had just changed back to blazing red flames and his fangs had elongated as he lifted Tom's jacket off the women who looked like she was just sleeping.

As soon as he lifted the coat, a river of blood flowed from her torn dress. She had a knife wound down her leg and her breathing was becoming faint. Molly was almost in a dream state that she would never wake up from.

"She needs a hospital now or she won't last the hour." King Artorik's deep raspy voice said as he looked back to the worried face of the Mayor.

"The nearest hospital is east and three hours away; she'll never make it." An older townswoman said in a whisper as she was still in shock.

King Artorik covered Molly back up and then gently held her in his arms. He flew wilder than a winter's breeze and faster that a humming birds wings carrying the fragile women to the hospital doors. He felt her lips kissing his abdomen and her fingers faintly caressing his muscles; which startled him into flying quicker. He knew this was the sweet goodbye for her husband she was dreaming of. He loudly sounded the hospital bell as he gently placed her so the nurses could find her. Then he waited one moment as the medical staff rushed out to take her in right away.

He then flew back equally as fast to find the crowd of people at the bank gathered around a sobbing Mayor.

Tom was crying; "My Molly; my only true love."

King Artorik's heart melted. His leathery bat-like-armor had lapsed as he remembered being that in love and finding out Guinevere was dead. But even his love of Guinevere had not compared to the love in this mortal's heart for his wife. He gathered Mayor Fields in his arms carefully; as the Mayor continued to cry into his chest.

King Artorik silently made a prayer to The Oneness that Molly would live so their love could be re-united in life. But if she didn't make it; he would make sure they were together in the afterlife. He slowly set the Mayor down at the hospital and the Mayor hugged him before rushing off to find his wife.

He had taken care of Tom and Molly but he had to help the other victims at the bank. He flew back and scanned the crowd. His red eyes found the other six women who had been tortured before Molly and flew each one to the hospital; sounding the alarm each time. Then he went back to the diminished and shocked crowd of people who had not moved from being so traumatized.

The King's clawed hand and hellish eyes waved over the crowd to get their attention and put everyone in a trance-like sleep. His deep, sternly voice spoke an ancient language of a forgetting spell that translated to; "You will forget the unspeakable evil you have witnessed tonight. Each one of you will only remember a stranger from out of town saved you from a madman."

Then he went and grabbed the madman's limp body. *What a tasty meal; a lovely stew these bones and meat will make.* He thought as he flew with the body back to the cave in the mountains. *I have done what I can and now I shall wait in my dismal abode for the armies of undead to rise up from hell.*

🌱🌱🌱🌱

CHAPTER 5

SHERIFF PENDRAGON

Three months had passed since the bank hold up and against King Artorik's better judgement he had stayed. Something deep in his soul had kept his wings stilled in the sanctuary of the cave and the community of the town. He couldn't leave them yet as he could feel the great evil coming. Maybe it would be tomorrow, or maybe it would be centuries from now but he would watch and wait until then. All he had was time. After all, what was an eternity to the King Demon of all vampires?

It was getting harder to just pop into town unnoticed as news had spread about the stranger rescuing members of the community. Then there were the stories of him not being human, but those were just rumors from the ladies he had rescued and forgot to compel. *The ladies haven't forgotten me. I can hear when they pray at night for me to come to them. Now that I know them more personally then I would have liked to. Dangerous is the flesh of the daughters of Eve.* He thought about these wicked thoughts and prayed for penance as the demon in him loved to eat human flesh but the man he used to be wanted to be enraptured in human flesh in very sinful ways. From this day forth he swore he would repent and stop using his charisma for charming the gentle ladies of the town. But with every glance of their eyes meeting his; it was an uncontrollable reaction. He was too irresistible to be mortal. So he would have to be stronger than the temptations of the world or else everyone would be in trouble; especially the married ladies who couldn't keep their hands off him.

He was gently rocking himself with his wings wrapping him tight as he clung to the cave ceiling. It was high noon and he was restless. He thought about when it was easier to just go for a bite. Three months ago he hadn't cared who the people were; his thirst was unquenchable. But now everything had changed. There was a devious part of him that wanted to make some women in town widows, but he buried those thoughts and the last lingering touches of secret moments by the river with a particular blonde maiden named Julia.

He referred to Julia as his river maiden and she was the one that kept his thoughts up all day. She was untamable. Something in her she-wolf spirit was as wild as the forest and lived for freedom. She had been widowed. He didn't have to kill anyone to take her.

Usually he was not in the nature of stealing affections from maidens without the intention of marriage. But he had become a beast in this modern day and age and some dangerous women had not cared about taking his virtue as he drank from them. But there was something about the river maiden; Julia was different. She was hard to resist and hard to obtain. And all he wanted to do was to own her heart. He kept thinking of her golden hair in the moonlight by the river. He couldn't control his temptation and would transform to a giant black wolf in trying to woo her. He wanted more of her. They had been secretly meeting every so many weeks and it was never enough.

As Pendragon divulged on his fantasy encounters with the particular golden haired maiden; he could hear trampling up the mountain like wild horses had crusaded up the landscape. He remained statuesque as the leaves rustling and twigs breaking got closer and closer to the cave entrance.

He immediately smelt the spicy oak scent of fancy cologne and then the strong floral scent of lavender slathered on thick of the soft skin it clung to. He knew it was Tom and the sweet smelling being was Molly. Molly had been the first human that he had ever carried to the hospital. She was also part of a very small handful of women; that he had not seduced and drank from. That night had been the first time in centuries since he had conversed with a small group of humans. His life up to this last century had been a never-ending cycle of coffee, hunting and blood baths. Sometimes losing himself in the lives he took. He had forgotten about what it meant to really live; or be a part of anything; or know anyone.

He sensed that Molly was healed. Both her heartbeats were weaker now. But she had fought to live and survived. Her human body was still fragile as she stepped forth into the entrance with Tom close behind and trying to pull her back. *What on earth is dragging them up the mountain to see a monster?* He thought as he kept his eyes closed while he listened to them stumbling around.

He breathed in deeply and filled his lungs with the cool scent of the cave and the aroma of moss, soil, and then...*was that desperation? Yes, a deep sadness and a scent of desperation is coming off of Molly's perfumed, sweat-clad body.* These thoughts of what he smelt off her skin stirred the human part left in his soul. It reminded him of every time he had drank the very last blood drop of his victims; clinging to their ordinary-pathetic lives. He sucked the sweetness of their wretched lives out of them; until their eyes were as dark as his. He mercilessly, drained them until their light had been extinguished.

"Hello? Pendragon? Are you here? This lovely lady by the river told us where to find you. Are you still here?" Tom Fields said as he followed Molly into the cave but managed to step in front of her.

Molly was now clutching his left arm with both her hands and her dress now revealed the growing baby bump. He listened to the rhythms of both beings in one body. There was some kind of magic that creates beings within a woman.

The two humans were treading on the crunching bones, dirt, and rocks on the cavern floor. An oversized rat scurried by them, partially running over Molly's high fashioned boots. The King dropped down as Molly was shrieking silently in her mind. He scooped up the juicy rat and bit off the head as the blood oozed out the sides of his mouth.

Tom and Molly both stepped back at the same time away from the shadowy figure that just dropped from the ceiling. His eyes were still glowing red as they listened to the sickening bones being crunched. Tom and Molly could now see his stature as the sunlight streamed through the opening of the cave and their eyes adjusted and small gasps escaped both their lips in sync.

King Artorik turned away from them almost as sudden as he had eaten the rat, and he could hear small gasps as they watched his wings retract. He quickly transformed back to his human-form. Then he wiped off his mouth and stretched. He could feel their eyes all over his body as he quickly jumped into his pants and then put on his favorite collared white shirt. He hadn't been accustomed to wearing clothes or manners in a very long time, and he could feel Molly's blushing gaze at his naked rippling torso. As he did up each button; he walked even slower until he stood about three feet apart from their rosy cheeks.

"Hello, Tom and Molly." As he said their names he intentionally hissed through his vampiric fangs not fully retracted but licked clean of the blood.

He looked up, casually closing his eyes and opening his mouth wide; slowly retracted his fangs to look about as humanly possible. He then blinked his eyes back to the gray-blue color that almost resembled human. In the light his irises held a soft red glow that couldn't be hidden. Fully transformed back to a human figure that was his natural regal handsomeness, he cleared his throat while intensely looking into Molly's eyes and listening to her lip biting scandalous thoughts.

"Sorry to have frightened you. I needed the snack. If I would have known you guys were coming I could have...decorated." King Artorik said warmly as he smiled and both men heard Molly sigh dreamily.

"Pendragon there is no way around this. You saved Molly and countless others that night at the bank. Right now we have a position of Sheriff that has opened up. We feel you could help keep our town peaceful, especially if there are more evil creatures that prey on the frailest victims of the community..." Tom said but held that same shiver in his voice from before and Molly untraditionally cut her husband's trailing words off and spoke directly to King Artorik.

She suddenly grabbed his cold right hand by her left hand and stepped closer to him locking their eyes as she placed his palm on her heart against her bosom. She was wearing the prettiest empress-waist, light blue dress King Artorik had seen in a long time. Her feathered hat was matching and held fresh lavender. Her opened petticoat held another lavender sprig pinned to the collar and Tom had a matching sprig in his overcoat. But none of that mattered as King Artorik was shocked at his cold hand now feeling her warm heart beating against his palm. He gasped as no one had ever dared take his hand in this manner before. He was surprised at her bravery and flattery. He knew this wasn't lust. *She is thanking me?* This thought stayed in his mind as her sweet voice spoke.

"King Artorik I apologize for being so untraditional. But I wanted to personally thank you for coming to my aid that terrible night. I begged Tom to drag me up to the mountain to see you. We knew you lived somewhere up here and then a lovely woman by the river told us where to find you. I just had to thank you with all my heart for saving my life. I know it is rash of me but I knitted this sweater for you to keep you warm up here on those darkest of nights. I just can't imagine being up here all by your lonesome." Molly said as a few tears streamed down her face and King Artorik had to clear his throat as she was warming his icy heart.

"Yes, as I was saying Molly before you interrupted me." Tom who was carrying a box under his arm handed it to King Artorik.

He hadn't even noticed Tom was carrying something as he took the box in both his unwilling hands and Tom sighed in relief that King Artorik's hand was now occupied by something other than his wife's bountiful heartbeat.

"Pendragon, the town and I would like you to be Sheriff on the midnight shift. You will be fully in charge from sun down to sunrise. We have a house for you. It was abandoned and we fixed it up for you. It is actually at the base of the mountain about a mile from a hidden trail to the old quarry. Can you please reconsider staying more permanently in our town? We would be forever honored and humbled by your presence." As Tom was speaking his voice still cracked.

King Artorik smiled at the words but he was more delighted with Tom's thoughts about how it would be a lot nicer to have such a protector on his side, instead of being a meal. Artorik held up the purple and yellow striped knitted sweater in the light.

In all his almost 1200 years of existence there had been only a few times where he felt purposeful. He had a grand purpose but a lot of the centuries he had slept through being deemed obsolete after the dark side was sent back to hell each time. But some centuries he had really enjoyed life; like fighting alongside Lancelot when they were like brothers.

He had always moved along with the centuries. He had only stayed long enough to vanquish the evil and to keep history guessing if the past events were truth or if they were fables. But the past didn't matter. The truth had become nothing more than bedtime stories or tales told around some campfire. He was the only thing left from the dark ages when dragons ruled the skies.

This Sheriff position would not be the noblest of efforts like the quest for the Holy Grail he had once obtained. But it did give him the chance to have a life again and a new smaller purpose. It also gave him the chance to be human again and try to fit back into society. *So what is it about this town that makes me compassionate towards the people in it? I have seen myself being ruthless for centuries. Why now? I can feel the magic of the mountain and the evil coming. It was what steered me here to begin with. The townsfolk really need help if they are ever to survive. Villains do make tasty meals, but so does drinking the river of despair pouring out of the generations of townsfolk.* As he thought these dark thoughts he looked up to their waiting expressions and grinned with his fangs extended.

"Okay Mayor Fields, but just for your knowledge; I am a creature bathed in dark magic and cannot be contained. So I will agree but on my conditions. Never question what I do with the heinous individuals I capture and that way your soul will be able to sleep at night. Let us shake on it and seal the deal." King Artorik said as his eyes glowed red while he put on his knitted sweater.

As he grinned he held out his hand and Tom took it; shaking it hard. The heat stung Tom's palm as their hand shake smoked. The deal really was sealed and unbeknownst to Tom; it was unbreakable.

❦❦❦

133 YEARS PASS BY IN THE BLINK OF AN EYE

🌾🌾🌾

CHAPTER 6

CALL ME MIDNIGHT

In keeping my promise to Mayor Fields; I had protected the town on the midnight shift for the last 133 years. Even though there had been nine Mayors since 1869. And even though the silver star burnt my flesh each day; I took great pride in pinning the Sheriff's badge on my chest. The name on my sleeve was stitched "Sheriff Pendragon" but everyone who lived in the town and knew me had nicknamed me *"Midnight"* and that suited me just fine.

History was too messy and too complicated for the humans to grasp. It was written down whom and what exactly I was; and given in a top secret file to each new Mayor over the years. But I wondered how much of my past the new Mayor had actually read. I wondered if the Mayor had read about that the fact that I was born in 700 A.D. and brought back to life after I died at the age of thirty-three. I wondered if the new Mayor knew how I saved Wallachia from the Ottoman Empire in the 14th century and ruled over all of Romania (not what the History books had described). Then I fought in the crusades, in the 16th century with the glorious knights as a brother in arms against the evil creatures in this world; only to be betrayed by the next ruling Pope and sentenced to burn at the stake.

The one thing that history had stayed true to time; was each century I had been betrayed and slaughtered; I had to disappear and start all over again. I had become a nomad for an eternity until coming to this village. And now I was much too powerful to be destroyed. My life after death was one big search for the next big evil to be vanquished and this little village had become a thriving town in the process of time passing.

Trenton had been booming with industry. Gone were the days of lumberjacks; fashionable petticoats and horse drawn carriages. Steal machines raced the paved streets as progress destroyed the earth to make the human's lives easier and more efficient. All the while time slowly dragged on; while I waited, watched, and ate the evilness in the town. *I have become the secret in a secret. I am the ever watchful Midnight Sheriff. I am the ghost in the darkness at the breaking of dusk and the town knows I am something supernatural, but no one dares question how come I have not aged in over eighty years. The new Mayor Woods can see the town council ledger through the last 133 years but I am the one name that has remained. I am the law. Tom must have given the key to the new Mayor. The key to a secret safe that holds the truth and the deal that was made with me. But every time Mayor Woods is around me; he avoids my eyes and cannot read the parchment paper again. I frighten him. I hope he doesn't do something stupid in his intimidation of me. I would hate to have to eat him. Then again...*It was three in the morning and I thought about time passing and thought about my old friend Tom Fields.

The new Mayor will have to accept me or else there will be dire consequences. Even though Mayor Woods has been the new Mayor for the last thirteen years; our relationship is fetchingly taxing. I wonder how long Mayor Woods' heart will last; hopefully, longer than the Mayor before him and the last Mayor before him.

It has been seventy-eight years since I visited the nursing home and Tom had made a last request in 1924. *I remember Tom's dementia was killing him and he was alone since Molly had passed years before. I took his life before he succeeded. My heart ached in drinking my human friends loneliness in his opium overdosed blood. It was a hard thing but it was better to save his soul from eternal damnation and kill him before the whole pill bottle stopped his heart beat.* I let that hurtful thought die with the memory of the old Mayor as I started cooking bacon and eggs in the little staff kitchen. Sometimes the past needs to stay in the past.

Breakfast was something I loved to prepare for my two favorite prisoners but I would keep to my strict diet. I could indulge in human food from time to time but it never fed my hunger.

As I cracked the eggs and watched the bacon start to sizzle; the aroma of breakfast was already filling the small jail. I could see the prisoner in cell number three shifting in a sobering sleep. As I glanced over to the tossing prisoner; I started singing an ancient lullaby to ease the distressed young man I had found being beaten in the alley again last night. *Let the sweetness of my voice sing you back to sleep my troubled child.* As soon as the song was finished I could hear the soft snores of peace.

🌾🌾🌾🌾

CHAPTER 7

JACK

He knew he shouldn't be looking. At this very moment if he was caught it would be instant death. He would die of total embarrassment. *I mean peeking at her through the bushes is wrong in itself. But she is just too beautiful to turn away. Come on Jack, get a grip boy. This is a bad idea.* His thoughts kept circling like a pack of wolves gnawing away at his conscious but he couldn't tear his eyes from her silhouette in the glow of the full moon.

It was a bright summery full moon the best of kinds when the heat of the night has a slight breeze off the water but not enough to keep the sweat from sticking to your butt. This wouldn't Matter because the water was deep enough to get lost in. Maybe that was why this quarry was banned to begin with instead of the old rumors of goblins in the mountains kidnapping teens.

He checked the location of the moon and noticed it was almost midnight. *What is this beautiful mystery lady doing at the quarry anyways? This is my thinking spot. The blue-green algae infested waters always leave a lingering smell all over my skin and I just can't get enough of that scent.*

Sometimes Jack would pretend he was a dolphin when the sun was high and the waters seemed to reflect some far-off tropical destination. It was the perfect escape he needed from the small-minded town.

And now this lady was standing there basking in the moonlight above him. There was only one way into the quarry and when he had come up the path; he was the only one that had remained. All the other teens had left and he had just stayed. There were only a handful of kids that came here anyways; not since the town had outlawed swimming in the quarry. It had been far too many moons since two kids had drowned and changed this once happy spot. The townsfolk blocked the road permanently and had even gone as far as hiding the entrance to erase the unfortunate event and prevent any future events from occurring.

The townsfolk thought witches had cursed the waters and goblins would eat any quarry trespassers. Yet it was always the same; anyone new in town was less than. What a world. It was such a shame too. When the sun was shining through the trees over the water, it was too dazzling for words. It was like a shimmer of magic. It was the magic of nature's brilliant peace. Its a private paradise away from the horrors of the townsfolk; away from the town period. Too remote to even hear if anyone was up here. And the seclusion was perfect for Jack.

But here she was standing on the rock that overlooked the waters far above him. He wondered what she was thinking about. From his vantage point he could clearly look up and see her staring at the moon.

She was on the giant flat rock that people trek up the mountain to climb out on the ledge and jump off of. In an attempt to prove their giant egos can tackle their catapulting fear.

The rock really was a true test of bravery. It was so high up, and the smooth surface had razor sharp edges. Then there was the quarry itself; so undeniably deep. But the rocks jutted out underneath and you really had to make a run for the clearance you needed to escape the rocks.

In the sunlight it was easy enough; but in the moonlight even as clear and as bright as the moon was; he prayed she didn't jump. He didn't want her to get hurt but he also had no intention of rescuing her. It's not that he didn't want to help. It was just that he was so used to being on the sidelines and a ghost. Jack was the teen that usually kept quiet and kept to himself. That was the only way no one would even know when he would secretly leave this town in his dust and go explore the world and find some happiness of his own. He dreamed of finding more creatures like him.

He could see her white nightie glowing with the soft light of the moon's rays. It was the kind of nightgown that looked like an old lady would wear; the kind that could double as a doily for a dinner table. *Hmmm...dinner; right, I'm so hungry.* He hadn't eaten yet. The task before her loveliness had come into the picture was actually hunting for rabbits and he had been until he spotted her.

Now he was breathless as he watched her haunting beauty. He was too fixated to stop gazing at her. Because as he was pondering about dinner she now had sparkles streaming down her face. He could see the silver lights streaming down her cheeks that twinkled as she wiped them away.

It was Azriella Astra from school. He had sat behind her in all his classes since she moved here. He still remembered her unique delicate floral scent whenever she passed him assignments and walked in front of him in the hallways. She was new in town. Stupid thing about small towns – everyone is new if you aren't born here.

She stopped wiping her cheek and started slowly undoing her

buttons. *Oh God.* He thought as he started blushing. Jack was eighteen and this was as close to any intimate moments he had ever had with any girl. *Oh no, what are you doing Azriella? Its midnight and good girls like you shouldn't be out skinny-dipping.* His thoughts dropped with her night gown.

She had these weird glowing vine tattoos all over her body; she was mesmerizing; so beautiful and in her pink lace underwear. Jack couldn't turn away as he could feel his heart racing and the moon calling him to howl. Something in her was triggering him to change again and faster than usual. He bent down on his hands and knees and tried to fight nature to watch her. Then he sensed her feelings. The sadness she had built up started making him cry. He had never seen someone so beautiful and so deeply sad.

She jumped. He watched as she didn't quite get clear of the rock. Maybe he was mistaken. He could see in the dark without the help of the moonlight but maybe he was wrong. How he hoped he was wrong. *Come up Azriella. Please, come up for air.* He kicked off his boots and jeans; throwing layers to the ground. In a moment he was in his boxers and jumped in.

The water was clear enough he could see her shadow sinking into the deep. He went for her and grabbed her hand. *Got her.* He thought as he pulled her so he could keep her head above the water. She had hit her head. The blood had left a trail and his eyes glowed inhuman red through the darkness. He noticed a small cut above her left eyebrow. She was so pretty and fragile, like a delicate flower wilting in a vase encased in the solidarity of the slightly crimson waters.

As he cautiously held her to keep her head above the water, he was thankful her eyes were shut because of his partial transformation. Very carefully, yet promptly, he swam to the shore with her and carried her to the grass. Swiftly he covered her with his laden t-shirt still sitting there in the moonlight. His cheek moved closer to her mouth as he held his breath and panicked when he couldn't feel her warm air being released on his skin.

Hastily, he did chest compressions and breathed life back into her. As his mouth touched her lips; she opened her mouth and coughed up water and he was shocked to see her luminescent yellow eyes staring back into his glowing red eyes. They both glowed even more towards each other and then she turned on her side closing her eyes once more. He quickly covered her up with his coat and used his discarded sock to stop the bleeding over her eye. It wasn't the most glamourous scene but he was using what he had.

He rapidly transformed into his beastly-self with four paws on the ground and ran like the wind back to the rock to fetch her nightie. It was the only way. He needed her to be okay and he needed to move faster than his inhuman bones could carry him. Animal instinct took over for one instant and he paused to stare at the moon in all its gloriousness. He lost control and let out a mighty blood-curdling howl at the moon. It was just too big of a moon to be wasted on heroism. He clenched her nightie in his oversized-fanged canines and ran in a worrisome gallop back to the fair damsel. As he ran back he wasn't certain if he seen a faint glow in his direction as he quickly transformed back to human and slipped on his pants. Although her eye lids remained closed; he placed his cheek to her mouth again to feel her breath on his skin and smiled in knowing she was okay.

Pragmatically Jack slipped her nightie back on and then his jacket back over her. She wasn't bleeding anymore; he had successfully stopped the blood but she was terribly cold and pale even with those strange tattoos faintly glowing. He gently lifted her in his arms and cradled her close to his heart; then started running as fast as he could. He had to get her to her grandmother's house. *What a paradox this is. Here*

I am the big bad wolf, bringing beauty back to her grandma's house instead of eating them both. Good thing I don't like the taste of teenagers. It's the excessive amount of cheeseburgers in their blood stream. I am more of a salad with a nice vinaigrette kind of werewolf anyways...But if she was a juicy rabbit. Focus there, easy boy. You'll hurt her if you transform with her in your arms...Focus. As his mind wandered as fast as his legs she stirred and he tried not to breathe too loudly as he ran faster.

Jack was more than grateful she lived on the outskirts of town down the long dirt road from his house. It was perfect for seclusion, except she did have more neighbors then him; three neighbors exactly three point three kilometers apart. Still at this late hour and through the brush he was sure no one would be around or awake. *God I hope Azriella is okay.* He thought as he held her closer to his chest hoping the heat from his skin would keep her warm. This wasn't the ending he wanted for her. He sensed her sadness and loneliness like it was his own.

"You'll be okay Azriella, please hang in there. We are so close to your home." Hugging her tighter he whispered.

His Dad had told him of the magic of this town and he had seen other worldly creatures but he wasn't sure what Azriella was. She was different from him. The glow of her golden eyes was brighter than the darkness in his soul. But he felt like she was like him; trying to fit into a human world. Being human was hard enough as it was. All he knew was this undying urge to protect her, and that love existed. His heart melted the moment his lips had touched hers to save her life.

The best course of action was to place her on the porch bench and ring the doorbell and disappear. His plan was solid because he sure didn't want to explain anything to her grandmother. She was a very scary old woman and reminded him of some wretched witch from a dark fairytale.

Gently he placed Azriella on the porch bench and re-covered her with his jacket. Faster than the beat of a hummingbird's wings he rang the doorbell and hid down in the bushes beside the porch steps. He was out of sight from the small window built into the closed door twenty feet away; but he could clearly hear the small approaching footsteps.

CHAPTER 8

JACK

He hoped that his eyes would stop glowing enough that he could remain hidden and still watch his sleeping princess on the porch bench being cared for by the person now creaking open the door.

"Jack Pendragon you better step out of the bushes right now or else." The decrepit voice came from behind him and filled him with astonishment because only a supernatural creature could be that stealth like.

Although Jack liked to think he was manly but the truth was this tiny old lady really scared the crap out of him. She looked positively spine-chilling. Her witchy crooked nose was just as pointy as her black hat that sat snug on her straw silver hair. *Where the hell did she come from?* His thoughts couldn't contain his shock either.

"Okay Grandma, you got me." Jack reluctantly said as he slowly turned so he could completely see his captor instead of side eyeing her.

He could sense the centuries off her weathered wrinkled skin and didn't want to turn predator on her. He literally just wanted to avoid any confrontations and start howling at the moon already. His true love was calling him and the juiciest of rabbits in Farmer Magland's field.

"Young man, why are you leaving Azriella there? I need you to carry her in, you big bonehead. Bring her up the stairs to her bed so I can take care of her." The scratchy old lady's voice hurt his ears like she was blowing a dog whistle and he squinted obeying her.

Gently, he picked up Azriella making sure his coat was still covering her and started trekking up the stairs. Instinctively he could smell which room was hers and which room was laden with mothballs. That same scent lingered on the old woman's hat like the wet basement smell that never seemed to leave an older house. He hadn't even realized Azriella's Grandma had followed him up. He watched the old woman quickly inspect her grandchild and kiss her cheek, while tucking her in.

"Thank you for bringing her home. She has been awfully lonely since moving here almost a year ago, after losing her mother. My name is Helga. I want you to stay and have tea with me." The old woman named Helga sounded more enchanted as she spoke.

Jack just nodded and followed her out Azriella's door. *Oh great here it comes. I'm busted and getting the third degree. All I did was save her life. Why is it always the good guy that takes the fall on these kinds of situations?* As Jack was rolling his eyes; his thoughts also included a little secret prayer that being chewed out wasn't going to take up too much time. He needed to get back to enjoying the moon.

But even as all these thoughts escaped he knew he couldn't just leave Azriella on the bench; he needed to know she was going to be okay. Something had burned his soul when her glowing eyes had met his. Even though they were different, he saw that kindred spirit full of magic and full of life. He was smitten as he remembered her eyes and his cheeks felt on fire with the blush that spread across his face. Her eyes had exposed her soul and showed him all her frailty. And she had given away a big secret. The eyes never lied and Azriella was just like him. She was trying to fit into a world where everyone different was some kind of monster. A small part of the world where people had hunted and slaughtered them until almost all the magical creatures were snuffed out of existence. The weird part that the townsfolk didn't realize was the hidden magic was completely surrounding the town. That was why his mother had come here so long ago. It was the one thing that kept them here. The magic in this town was like an unstoppable magnet drawing other magic inwards.

But the townsfolk themselves were a particularly cruel and odd bunch of humans. *The community is unabashedly cruel towards anyone who isn't born here. Anyone that is an outsider is immediately an outcast. Maybe it is because of the centuries of concealed magic that occasionally slips out. The town had blamed witchcraft for everything that had gone wrong in their lives. Mostly, the community had just fallen on hard times. With no innovation Trenton couldn't hope to begin again. Thank goodness for that new Mayor that purchased the mine and started drilling again; or else the town would have easily become a ghost town.* As these thoughts were swirling around him a tea pot floated past his head and started pouring tea in a china cup that magically appeared before a drop was wasted.

"Jack would you prefer one sugar or two? Or maybe you would like the tea black; like your rich wretched heart? Just teasing; young child of the moon." Helga laughed a cackle of a laugh that made the tiny hairs on Jack's neck stand up.

Jack knew Azriella was magical and so logically her Grandma was too but he just didn't know what kind of creatures they were. He just sat there a little stunned about the floating teapot, but smiled at the fine china and the small icebreaker joke she had made. *My heart may be black but I'm not evil. In fact, I care about my soul and the preservation of life in general; except for those abundant tasty rabbits that I am forbidden to eat.* Jack thought as he looked at the strange tea swirling in the china cup.

"Drink up Jack. This will keep you warm especially after your midnight swim." Helga said sharply and Jack almost spit out his tea at her intuition.

Immediately he panicked but kept it contained as he slurped his tea unusually loud and resisted the urge to spit across the table. *Uh oh, she knows. But how much she knows is the real question? I don't have time for this; the moon is calling and I need to feel the wind through my fur. And I need to feel the grassy dew against my running paws. I need freedom and I need blood. I need the iron. I need to feed. The moon won't let me contain my urges for too much longer.* Jack thought as he drank more tea while Helga watched him.

"I have just given you a potion." Helga said.

"Why?" Jack gasped.

"You need to listen to what I have to say. You will always be protected by the forces of the fae and the light of magic for what you have done for my granddaughter. You have saved her life. I had seen the other reality of her life ending; if it hadn't been for you. The vision had come to me and then I saw her future change before my eyes with you breathing life back into her." Helga cleared her croaky throat and paused while Jack looked at his empty cup fearful.

"I know you my dear. You are a noble werewolf. I admire your compassionate traits and courage to bring her to me and to stay for tea. But you have to forget about Azriella. The tattoos you saw on her skin should never have been viewed by your kind. Your knowledge of those marks is what would put your very life in danger. There has been a war since the dawn of time. It is a great battle with the sons of light against the sons of darkness. Pure evil will seek you out now because of that knowledge and the power it holds. It is foretold a great warrior will have to vanquish and protect the fae people when the time comes. It is foretold that the next Fae Queen will fight in the battle and help in overcoming the darkness; restoring the balance of peace in the earth. It will be a new world where magical and non-magical beings can coexist together." She spoke and her eyes changed to a purple that glowed and he felt instantly like his skin was on fire.

"Jack, you have to forget about my granddaughter. Azriella needs to focus on her duties and destiny; the Fae King will choose her to rule our kingdoms because of her warrior skills. She is royalty doesn't need some handsome, lower species ruining her life and future." Helga's tone and words cut him deeply.

Jack wasn't angry but that remark cut. *Lower species? I am the son of a great King and a Prince. We are all of the same magic.* Deep down he knew it. *Can't she feel the royal energy of magic in me?* He was shocked because he had never expected to be rejected by another magical creature. Jack knew he could be a rogue at times; but also knew when it was time to leave. His head was spinning. He looked at the empty tea cup and the tiny painted rabbits were moving and dancing. The rabbits were also laughing at him...*little jerks.* He thought as his supernatural hearing picked up on the laughter from the cup. He thought he could even hear the rabbits laughing outside from the bushes. Or maybe that was the tea? *I have to leave this place.* He was starting to worry as he stumbled away from the table and tried to make it to the opened front door; clutching the frame tight.

"Don't worry you will forget this night. In moments you will be back to yourself; barking at the moon and forgetting you even saw Azriella. I hope I made the tea strong enough that you both will forget about each other completely." Helga cackled but stopped abruptly as his fangs extended and he looked over to her with eyes crimson and glowing.

Jack was thinking like a madman. Maybe it was the tea, or the burning desire in his heart to really kiss Azriella and marry her. Wolves mated for life and now this old woman was severing his connection with Azriella. He wouldn't even get to know his heart's desire in a few minutes. Random thoughts were swirling through his head; *Azriella do you love the moon like I do? Do you like doilies? Because I sure do.* Everything he would never get the chance to ask her.

He became so heartbroken he started trembling with a secret rage that he had never known before. He stomped out of the house leaving the door wide open. Helga came to the door worried about what her magic was doing and how she hadn't factored in the proper dosage when werewolf love was involved. Her eyebrows were crinkled high with worry as she watched his back arch and his head cocked to the moon.

"Since, I am such a lower species anyways Helga." His voice was raspy and deeper than before.

He whipped off his pants and transformed; mooning her in the process.

"My heavens, Jack!" Helga shouted in anger while watching him pee on her magnolia tree in the front yard.

"Thanks for the tea." He growled and then started running as fast as he could.

"Jack Pendragon I never want to see you again around here. Do you hear me? You are just trouble through and through." Helga had shouted after him and spoke the last words in frustration.

"Thank goodness he's gone. Damn it, I owe him a life debt but I don't have to like the cheeky meathead. Frig, he took the teacup. His magic can't be that powerful yet? I wonder if he knows the prophesy and that his Dad is this planets ticking time bomb?" Helga asked herself as she made a new pot of tea and pondered things she shouldn't speak aloud or else the demon would come for her.

She made herself a promise to keep but knew it was no good to delay destiny as all their paths were changing. But she would still try. *Great, now there is going to be all this trouble because that young man is going to be in our lives. Well, I will just have to keep putting magic spells over him and keep destiny from happening. Just great a werewolf for a grandson-in-law; what is the world coming to? Right, it's the end.* Helga thought as she dipped her biscuit in her tea. Tonight she knew she was eating the whole damn bag because destiny was coming for them all and her time had passed. She was too old to partake in the war this time. The future was for the youth if they were brave enough to hold onto it and fight for their freedom.

🌿🌿🌿

CHAPTER 9

JACK

Jack's huge jagged teeth were ripping into a leg of the juicy rabbit he had captured. *Thank you Universe, for this sustenance.* He thought as he lay on his back on the flat rock, completely content for the moment. But then he started to become worrisome as he thought about how he actually got here. His memory didn't reflect the last couple of hours; or even when he had caught the succulent rabbits he was eating. And above all else; he had a tea cup with him. *For crying out loud; I have no clothes but some weird crystal tea cup. What happened to me?* His thoughts were troublesome but he continued to munch.

He started gently squeezing the rabbit's eye balls in his mouth. They reminded him of squishy bouncy balls. He hated the fact that it was a dog mentality and he was a great wolf. But he still loved squeezing them in his canines until they popped out the lovely juice.

His heart was sad and he didn't know why. He quickly moved onto the next rabbit. *Great, now I am binge eating on rabbits. Why am I so depressed? This is the life. I have everything I need right here in the quarry. The moon loves me and I love her; so why do I feel so alone.* Maybe it was something more he thought as he looked at the strange tea cup that held painted dancing rabbits all over the china. He let out a heartbreaking loud howl. Then he howled again. He wanted the moon to feel his loneliness. He even let his tears flow. *Why must I spend eternity alone? Is it because I was born into darkness?* He stopped his pity party for a moment when the wind picked up and he smelt something delightful on the rock. The scent made his heart skip. He sniffed and breathed in the scent; creating a space for it in his memory. It was a lovely female scent. Something about the smell lingered in his brain and in his heart. He didn't know why but the smell comforted him and gave him hope. The smell was strong enough that he knew whoever she was. She had been there maybe a couple of hours before. He jumped off the rock and into the cool abyss.

He shook off as he got on the bank of the quarry's slick grass. He immediately started sniffing. He could smell foot prints. But he had absolutely no memory of going swimming tonight, let alone meeting a beautiful stranger of the lady persuasion

Jack was happy at least. Or so he thought. But slowly the missing pieces of his memory started taking over a panic of what had happened tonight. There was a jigsaw of glimmers of fuzzy memories that he couldn't find the forms of what had happened. The last time he had blacked out, he had awaked in some old hag's cabin and she was going to make a wolf barbeque sandwich out of him. Good thing he escaped when he did. Being captured by a lady sure seemed fun at the time but not if she was going to consume his magical soul. Thank heavens his claws were sharp and he could transform anytime he wanted. Her heart had been a bitter taste of the world and when he had torn into the muscle he tasted her loneliness too and it made him well aware of his own. But it gave him a good meal. Plus she had all kinds of candies, and gingerbread around the cabin to snack on.

Away from those memories and back to the familiar scent he had been circling with his nose on the grass. He could smell his own scent and this flowery creature-human. *Yes, it was definitely a lady; possibly a human.* He could see that the mysterious woman had been lying down lengthwise by the signs of the flattened grass. And he could tell that he had been knelling beside her; possibly over her by the way the grass was flat and circular.

His nostrils caught something darker on the grass. The dark crimson liquid covered his nose and his giant wolf tongue licked it off. *It is her blood and it isn't human.* Although he could definitely drink her floral scented blood, like it was some herbal tea. But it wasn't his thing; rescuing damsels and then eating them.

Jack could smell her scent all day; it was as intoxicating as running through the woods. He would be quite happy to be by her side for all eternity; just in her presence where he could smell her orchid of loveliness. *I was starving before these rabbits. So I had to have been helping her. Eating humans is so filling plus nauseating. Maybe I was helping her because she was injured?*

It was at this moment Jack wished he had worked just a little harder on his wolf senses instead of hanging with his friends and playing video games. He had passed down a few hunting trips and now nature's instinct was harder to use. There just wasn't a werewolf 101 class in his high school. *Screw it. I need more rabbits. This unsolvable night and mystery lady will have to wait.* He thought as he looked into the shadows of the forest around the quarry.

Across the glade he could see the moonlight shining through two beacons under a bush. And his immediate attention snapped like a light switch turned on to the thought of squishing bouncy balls with his fangs.

🌿🌿🌿🌿

CHAPTER 10

JACK

Jack could smell the scent of outdoor fresh fabric softener and some freshly picked daisies beside the night side table. His eyes fluttered to the open cell door and then far across the room where a uniformed figure was frying bacon. He could hear the sizzling and could smell the maple flavor. He knew immediately where he was as the figure with tinted shades stiffened and turned to look over. The figure smiled warmly with bigger than life fangs as their glasses magically slid down their nose so Jack could see the red demon's happy eyes.

"Ah, finally awake Mr. Pendragon." The deep eerie voice was inviting as the Sheriff's eyes looked to Jack and then to the table.

Jack sat up moving the millions of blankets placed on top him and grabbed his aching head that felt like it was going to explode.

"What happened?" His voice was weak as he swung his socks over the edge of the bed and stood up to stretch.

"Jack, I know you teenagers get partying but I always thought of you as a good young adult. Seriously kiddo, you gotta stop passing out naked in farmer's fields. I don't know what you were into last night but I had to carry your dead-weight to the truck and then to the bed in the holding cell. And you didn't wake up once. Have you any idea what time it is? Its 2:30am buddy; the sun will be up in a couple of hours. What if I hadn't found you?" Sheriff Midnight's stern voice sent chills down Jack's spine as he sat down at the table and was served bacon and eggs.

"You always find me." Jack said while almost inhaling the food even though his head still hurt.

"Well it's a good thing. You were panicking all the woodland creatures. I can only imagine the therapy they are going to need in seeing two moons last night. You are lucky I have been keeping extra clothes for you in the patrol truck. As you can see I have adorned you in the latest fashion of a white tee and blue jeans. And I knew you'd be ravenous so I made some extra bacon. There's some orange juice and some toast with strawberry jam there for you too."

"Those woodland creatures are weak, besides it's not the first time." Jack said and chuckled.

"Yes, and it won't be the last. I'm positive about it. I received a complaint from that sweet old lady on Elm Street. You know that family is new in town and they don't need any trouble. We both know what it is like being new." The Sheriff said in his supernatural voice as his red eyes deadlocked with Jacks.

Sheriff Midnight slowly took off his shades while sitting across from Jack. Jack could see there was another container jug that held what looked like a red smoothie that the Sheriff was slurping threw a straw making Jack queasy and wince at the container.

"Don't worry; this is no one you know." As Sheriff Midnight

smiled wide his fangs were still bright red with the thick liquid.

"But you need to start doing something more productive with the life you were given Jack. You are too smart to be still eating drug induced rabbits from Farmer Magland's farm. So get off the rabbits so you can graduate high school. Make a good go of it, okay? I would hate to see something happen to you my little wolf. And I don't want to slaughter the whole town if something does. Please be careful." Sheriff Midnight's voice was rough and supernatural but Jack had heard the gentle change of tone even though it was inhumanly subtle.

Jack helped himself to more bacon and nodded in silence as they just looked at each other reflecting on years of memories through each other's thoughts. This was how most dinners went in the Pendragon household but Jack was glad he had two parents always there for him; even if one really would kill and eat the whole town if something happened to him.

☘☘☘☘

CHAPTER 11

MIDNIGHT AND JULIA'S STORY

Midnight had told the story so many times that Jack could recall pieces of the puzzle in his brain of the very day his Mother had met the lonesome King by the river in 1869. Midnight's thoughts were taking a trip down memory lane with his Son as they sat there eating in silence.

Most humans don't know about the magical world and how slowly it ages; that was why magic was passed down and taught to families for the use of specific spells of protection. Forgetting Spells were needed because how else could anyone explain the obvious non-aging of certain people in town. Most humans didn't know about the laws of the magical world and how supernatural creatures weren't allowed to be with different species of magical creatures. No one knows who made these rules except they were followed by most, except the immortal who was born before the rules were ever invented.

♨♨♨♨

Julia had already been in her thirties when she had met me; the King Demon of Avalon and all Vampires. She was unfashionably independent for the 18th century and a beautiful mystery to me. She was a true lone wolf never wanting to settle down in those days. But she had captivated my heart by the river the day she had tried to save my life before she felt my cold lips. And even though years had passed and it was now the year 1986; she was ageless and I had stopped aging. We were crazy for each other but we had made a secret pact not to ask questions and interfere with each other's personal lives. We are both supernatural but our love was forbidden and Julia refused to open her heart further to me. Then she disappeared suddenly for almost two years and I felt like I had lost my secret friend forever. Each day was becoming drearier going into work knowing she wouldn't be there when I got off my shift.

I knew she was my soulmate from the start. But what cemented our relationship to more than riverside kissing acquaintances was one fated night when I received a frantic phone call from the famous Farmer Magland.

Old Farmer Magland was known across three county lines as being notorious for winning every vegetable competition. He grew absurdly large prized veggies and everyone was dying to know his secret although he attributed the success due to his prize winning horse manure pile. But what everyone didn't know was that he had always had one true passion that lit a fire in his soul and it wasn't his fancy gardening.

The farmer's true love was chemistry. After years and years of experimenting he had caught a lucky breakthrough in developing a very toxic, special plant food. The result was giant vegetables the size of small dogs; this also included pumpkins the size pregnant cows.

The side effects weren't as glamourous as all the ribbons and trophies. But that never stopped people from buying his wares at the local market. Any of his veggies gave you at least two of the following symptoms; diarrhea, nausea, black outs; double vision; hypertension and temporary blindness. Unless you had been eating the plants regularly and developed a tolerance (which took many years); you'd be in big trouble for the next couple of days.

Out of towners would continue to have problems but no one ever considered that the vegetables did it. No one knew the truth. Farmer Magland had taken food poisoning to a whole other level and made himself filthy rich in the process. But since the small town of Trenton never changed, the locals had developed two generations of tolerance to the poisoning. So they loved Farmer Magland. In fact, he was their hero. He had given them *wholesome* food that could feed large families on a poor man's budget.

The other side effects of the toxic plant food included any rodents that snacked turned enormous too, but also died horrible deaths. There was only one exception; one woodland creature had developed years of a tolerance and held the toxin in their veins to prove it. The cottontails in this area feasted on all of the veggies and grew abnormal in size.

The rabbits had a steady diet of nuclear plant food and some were obscenely larger than the vegetables themselves. Farmer Magland knew the giant size of the rabbits and set bear traps across his property. He disliked the bunnies so much because they were the evidence against him if anyone should ever pin the toxin back to the veggies and his farm.

The large white wolf had been feasting on the giant rabbits and became disorientated. The graceful creature of the night had been stumbling and got caught terribly in the bear trap in the middle of Farmer Magland's field. The howling agony was eerie as the morning fog set through the forest and I heard the wolf's howling cries from across town.

That was when Farmer Magland called me. I could even smell the fear dripped sweat down the farmer's back from over the phone. The farmer had needed me to do the dirty work and take care of the injured wolf. I could hear the sickening gleam in the farmer's voice about how the wolf had been trampling around the garden eating rodents and stepped on the old bear trap that was accidently left there. I could hear the secret desire of the farmer's happiness that the wolves were stepping in to rescue his prized vegetables. Except this wolf that had threatened to destroy his whole existence. There was going to be too many questions with this dead wolf not to mention the illegal bear trap.

The magnificent white wolf had been staggering back and forth when I strolled across the field towards it. I could see the farmer watching me as my red eyes glared at him. The farmer was smiling and it disgusted me but there was only one thing to do. I raised my gun at the growling wolf and pulled the trigger.

I remember my shallow breaths had stopped as I saw the majesty of the moonlight surrounding her. Even as I aimed my long barrel at the creature again and pulled the trigger; it was like I couldn't remember how to fake breathe. I couldn't remember anything as I looked at the magnificence of the beast that finally dropped. Here was my fellow creature of the night. Here was my secret friend for over sixty years that I had just shot.

The cries were dying as I approached for one more hind quarters shot. As I pulled the trigger again; she finally was out. I walked over to carefully re-set the bear trap claw and took her sweet paw out of the trap. Then I crumpled the metal like a tin can so the farmer would never use the cruel trap again on any other animal. The giant she-wolf had been very badly injured.

Then this tiny black wolf pup comes out of the long grass. The small pup yelped as it went to the fallen giant she-wolf. I exhaled a sigh of relief that I had listened to my unfailing gut and used the elephant tranquilizers instead of the bullets the Farmer wanted me to plow into the wolfs chest. The tranquilizers had saved the day another time too when a bunch of goblins were harassing the miners.

I carefully carried the she-wolf to my patrol truck and the little pup followed me, biting my heels the whole way. The little pup was crying in hot pursuit of the man who was carrying its mother.

I placed the giant wolf on the front seat and helped the scrambling pup get into the vehicle. *This little baby smells familiar but I can't place my finger on it.* The more I looked at the little beast that was still crying; the more the little pup tried to snuggle the unconscious mother. The little pup's glowing eyes had flashed a familiar red in anger and then changed to a gray-blue. *What do I know about child rearing? If this was the Cerberus of old, I would just play wrestle the beast and be on my way. But what do I do with a baby? For that Matter what am I going to do with this mother wolf? Wolf blood is good but not in this condition. Think...you primeval Windbag. Think. What do I do with these beautiful creatures?* My thoughts were scattered and I contemplated killing them both for peace of mind. But as I drove off with one hand on the steering wheel; my other hand was trying to hold a black fuzzy wolf pup licking and biting me.

I had fallen smitten to scratching behind the little cashmere pups ear. *How I miss the finer things in life and the palace. That was a time of centuries when I had the best of everything. My life now has become a meaningless pursuit of devouring evil. I missed out the first time on a true family. And here I have a second chance. She is here now; my friend that I've shot. Some hero of the people, I've turned out to be.* His thoughts drifted to the giant sleeping wolf that started snoring as the very tiny pup yawned and fell asleep on its back.

She was the same wolf; my river maiden that had fed me when I was in desperation. *Now I know why she had disappeared over the last two years.*

All the wolves in this town had intrigued him because they were a rowdy bunch. But she was different. Even though I had moved from the cave to a small home in the countryside on the very outer limits of town; I could see her sometimes in the trees of my property and smell her intoxicating scent in the air. There was something about her. I had even transformed to be with her several times. My black coat and teeth were more demonic than any other wolf but still we would run and frolic in the forest together ending up by the river. *Wolves mate for life, no Matter how much the darkness consumes my soul. She is mine. And they are mine.*

The wolves were as much as an enigma as the other creatures of this town. They were part of the ebb and flow of magic surrounding this place. *Here I am the Sheriff called in to shoot this beautiful darkness from a farmer who poisons us all. I should go back and drain that scallywag's life.* Even though my thoughts raged and my eyes remained a merciless red; I continued to drive to the station. I had carefully carried the giant wolf like a baby in one arm and with the other arm carried the biting pup that was growling. I used magic to shut the truck doors and open the stations doors. The jail always sat empty because if you were evil there wasn't a body left to prosecute.

I set the little pup on the floor while I put the giant wolf on the big station lunchbreak table. Then I scrambled for the first aid kit and alcohol to clean the wound. I had contemplated licking the wound clean but I knew that this wolf was drugged higher than a kite and didn't want to be high as I carefully shaved around the area and stitched the long jagged wound. *Poor thing; I hope she can heal.* I remembered thinking as I had wrapped her foot and leg. *If this was three hundred years ago I would have just ripped Farmer Magland's throat out instead of giving him a fine. Obviously, the wolf was eating the rabbits not the prized pumpkins. Boy was I glad I destroyed that bear trap but no doubt he has a hundred more on that sketchy piece of property he owns.* The more my thoughts consumed me with revenge on the farmer the more I stroked the giant wolf's fur as I looked back and forth to her; and the wolf pup that had pulled off my jacket from the chair to the floor.

The pup was very tiny but managed to bite into the uniform jacket; ripping it and then snuggling with it. I could see the little creature sniffing the collar and then passed completely out from exhaustion. As I relished in the thought of killing the farmer; I exhaled deeply. My shift was almost over as I made up my mind and wrote a note to the Deputy that would change my future forever.

"Well now. I guess we are all going home. My little goons can run this station as we are taking a family vacation for the first time in my existence." I remember whispering to my two sleeping wolves.

I used my powers to open the doors as I carried them both back to my truck and speed off to home. I remembered being so excited I almost ran a red light and almost forgot to lock the station back up. My thoughts were on long runs in the woods and hunting as a pack.

As soon as my she-wolf was healed we were going to have family fun. But first she needed a bath her coat smelled like the filth of the toxic farm. I didn't have any reservations about her attacking me. I was her Alpha but the pup had no idea who I was or what I was. *That's going to be tricky. But the baby will grow to love me. I mean who doesn't love the King of Darkness? I like the ring of that term the locals gave me.*

Daylight was coming as we entered my abode and I carried them both down to the medieval dungeons were my lair was. It was specially crafted out of old castle stone and there was a room specifically for my coffins and chests filled with healing soil from Avalon and Wallachia. I hadn't needed to use the healing coffins in a long time because I was much stronger now.

Over the years I had upgraded my abode with a queen sized bed in my room and a private bathroom with a giant underground lagoon for bathing in. I even had an empty spare bedroom down the stone hallway that had been sitting empty for years. As if I could ever keep company for that long…Alive. The finer things I had acquired included fine linen but I had kept the flame lit torches for the dark gloomy stone hallway. The torches had always made me feel like home and after existing for 1284 years I needed that flamed peacefulness; even though it was the year 1984.

The little pup had not stirred as it softly snored when I placed it on my bed still wrapped in my jacket. Then I carried the sleeping giant wolf into the lagoon area. I gently placed her down as I went into the refreshing blue-green waters. The water was fed by a rejuvenating spring from the mountain which filled the lagoon and then recycled flowing back out being cleaned naturally by the salmon that were in the bottom of the blue-green waters. It was my own creation and another creature comfort I needed. This little oasis was my sanctuary from the world and the salmon were of a magical kind of healing substance; if I chose to eat them.

Jeeves had prepared everything for me, like always. I sat down in the warm shallow edge of the water grabbing the shampoo and lathered her up very gently washing. And ever so carefully I rinsed her silky coat even using a brush to comb out any matted fur.

Jeeves was the magic in the cavern and waited on my every need; I only had to think once about what I needed and it already appeared before the thought even gave shape. It was something that is tuned into my soul; like a dial on the radio automatically in sync. When I constructed this little part of my sanctuary; it had been here waiting. It was calling out to me when I placed my treasure chests and even before I dug the first hole to tap into the spring. The magic clings to its master that had freed it from the earth. It is an invisible entity that worships the ground I fly over. The magic hovered as it held her so I could dry her off. The magic as if it is an invisible butler held another towel and some boxers for me. I ended up nicknaming the beloved magic Jeeves; as it grew to be a part of the family. I placed my bride in my bed and immediately the little pup instinctively moved to her. As I climbed in I fell asleep with my arm around her.

As soon as I saw you Jackie Boy I knew I wanted to have you both for all of eternity. But it wasn't until that first night I had made up my mind Jack; that you were both mine. And I was determined to win your mother's heart at all costs. And as you know I never lose.

❦❦❦❦

I woke up the next day and she was still sick. I cared for you while she slept and then it was the next day that she opened her large yellow eyes to mine and I was relieved. Your mother had looked at me in such pain it broke my heart.

"Just one moment Darling, I will bring you something to eat." I remembered speaking coarse but softer than I had ever spoke to anyone in my existence next to you Jack.

That day you had been swimming with Jeeves and he was watching you; so I could scoop handfuls of blood into your mother's mouth. She was so sick she couldn't lift her head. I called in to work and took weeks off. While you were having fun with Jeeves swimming in the lagoon and eating raw beef livers; your Mother had been struggling to live.

It was an incredibly slow process but I stayed stoic as I took care of her; gently placing her head on my chest so I could scoop blood into her mouth. Until gradually she started being able to lift her head and nurse you Jack.

As she grew in strength so did her slight growls; but mistrust then became trust as she knew I was taking care of you both. I would take her to the backyard as she growled placing her by the garden under a large oak tree. It was easier to show her I was taking care of her by transforming into my giant black wolf-form when it was dusk. The closest neighbor was miles away, so I didn't think twice about transforming to the wolf that she recognized. I was the Alpha that she knew for many years.

I would disappear into the woods but look back to see her ears perked and her eyes fixed on me. Then I would came back a moment later still watching her eyes that never faltered but grew more intense as I approached her with a deer. My prance was like that of a pony and not of the giant black demon-wolf as I paraded in front of her before placing the deer in front of her paws.

I changed in front of her back to my human form so I could rip into the juicy tendons and hand feed her the meat in smaller pieces. I watched as her eyes grew wider and a shocked expression came all over her predator face. I had seen this wonder and amazement for hundreds of years by adoring women who loved every inch of my muscular body. I had been worshipped by many but none of that compared to her giant gaze at me.

Years of immortality had made me unabashedly free with my different forms in all their dark beauty. Eternal creatures are never prudish and I deliciously feasted on her eyes all over my large spectacular body. *Dad we can skip over that part.* Jack's thought interrupted the story. *Alright but as long as we both know how spectacular I really am.* My thoughts answered back and then continued the story.

❦❦❦❦

She got better daily so I had re-introduced her in small doses to rabbits again so she could develop a poison tolerance.

I remember saying to her; "This is the very thing which made you sick. But it is also the thing which will cure you. The more you eat, the more tolerant your body will adjust to the poison chemicals. Then you can be free to hunt in the woods and never fall ill again. Most of the smaller animals feast in Farmer Magland's field and all of the larger animals, in return, feast on them. When we go hunting together we will have no limitations on what we can eat."

I had re-assured her she was safe as we ate together. You were getting bigger and bigger; and I took off even more time from work, as your Mother slowly healed.

I remember the first time she had took the meat from my hand; it made my heart feel warm and fuzzy. Very uncharacteristically of me as I always wanted to dominate everyone and everything even if I did have a fancy for saving the humans from darkness. But this was different. I remember seeing her excitement growing slightly as she snapped bubbles and her tail started wagging.

Each time I would place her in bed before dawn and transform back to my big wolf-form so we could snuggle as a pack. I remember thinking even now; so *this is living. Who in Hades would have thought that I could be this happy in my 1284th year on this planet? I never could have dreamed that a King demon vampire such as myself could be so completely happy with a 200lbs. werewolf and our little baby werewolf.*

This bliss was never ending and continued as her spirits lifted and her paw healed. Then I heard the fluttering thoughts of her mind. She couldn't transform back to her true-self yet as she was still unhealed but she wanted to. It was becoming clear any night she might transform in front of me. I could sense her shyness, even though I had seen her many times by the river and in my dreams. But I could also feel her sadness. She felt like she had betrayed me even though she hadn't.

I remember one time you had come over to me as a curious pup when I was in wolf-form and I smelt the top of your head. I deeply inhaled your essence and my breath got stuck in my throat as I truly looked at you and our matching black coats. I let out a long concise howl and you both howled with me. I remembered thinking; *this really is my family. I didn't even think it was possible for me to have children. But here I am looking at my werewolf baby. But Julia has always been my wife from the first moment I caught her bathing in the river in the moonlight.* I remember the more I reflected on my thoughts and the events of our secret love; and then read her human-fears and heart whispers; the more I felt like I was losing myself. *Actually now in reflection on the whole situation, I was quite sure I had lost my soul but this time it wasn't to darkness. It was a different kind of hell and I knew that I might lose my light if I ever lost you both. The blood thirst was one thing but to have lost what I just found. I had gained something so invaluable to me that no amount of treasure in the world could compare.* The agony would drive me insane and I really would go and do the Devil's bidding. *This is the most dangerous situation, indeed.* My thoughts interrupted the memory I was telling Jack for one moment and then I continued to tell my love story.

🌲🌲🌲🌲

Finally the day came when your Mother was healed. Jeeves said he would look after you while I took your Mother into the woods for a good hunt. We were going to get bear and we drove for miles and miles out into the deepest part of the wilderness off a little unmarked road.

I could hear her thoughts about being so happy; she adored the man who saved her life. There was no way she could fend off any predators in the weaken state she was in or worse the farmer could have just killed her.

That day she was finally healed we were practicing as a pack in the daylight. Although I was in my vampiric-form and she was in her giant wolf-form; we had great success as she flanked the outside and corralled the prey. Together we took down the grizzly and ate vigorously. My thoughts were of pure happiness as we tore into the flesh of the mammoth killer.

While we were eating the shots came out from under the canopy of trees. I hadn't been under attack in such a long time that I was totally caught off guard as I took a round of slugs in the back and even more as I turned around; the culprit continued to unload their automatic. I remembered watching in sadness as my beloved wolf fled into the woods as I sat against a large oak while the blood poured out of the holes throughout my collared shirt. I remembered thinking; *great this is going to take forever to heal from. But when I am healed I will track down this rebellious energy and they shall regret the day they dared to gun me down.*

Then I saw my beloved she-wolf come back with a human arm attached to the machine gun in her mouth. She rushed to my side and dropped the arm at my feet.

"I knew you would not leave me at this distinguished inconvenience of unruly attitudes and prejudices against vampires. Society is so uncivilized to my kind, but not you my Darling. You came back for me." I remembered saying in my deep demonic voice as blood continued to rush out of all the holes in me.

I watched her try to lick the wounds and I placed my hand up to stop her.

"My Darling, I appreciate the gesture but my blood would change you. I need fresh blood to heal fast or else I shall be here until tomorrow morning with all the silver that has entered my body." I remembered saying to her in serious agony.

"Thank you for not leaving me." I said as I tried to act brave sticking my chin up and my chest pouring blood out.

Then I will never forget as I sat against the tree and she turned from me crouching down and transformed in front of me to my beautiful, river maiden; my secret lover.

"How could I leave the one I love? Please drink from me and heal so we may leave this place." Her moonlit voice was sweet and sultry as were her bountiful curves in the summer sunlight.

I was in awe. My jaw had fallen on the forest floor along with the drool as I witnessed her beauty and heard from her the words I wanted to hear from her so many times. *She loves me.* My beautiful maiden was in fact a gorgeous werewolf. Her delicate arm and hand healed from the treacherous trap. Now she offered her hand and I took it gladly. I kissed her hand before pulling her into my arms and kissing her sweetly. I licked and kissed her neck before tenderly biting her as she softly moaned. The bullets moved out of my skin and shredded shirt; almost all at once as my golden skin even sealed.

I looked upon everything I had missed upon seeing these last couple of years when she had disappeared. I only took the blood I needed from my love; and gently lifted us both in the air. As I touched back down on the earth; I continued to embrace her as I faced her sweet smile and closed eyes. I licked her neck where the fang puncture holes were and instantly they sealed.

"Thank you Julia for saving my life that day you stepped on that bear trap." I remembered saying to her quickly unbuttoning my shirt and placing it on her; re-buttoning as she was stealing kisses.

"I saved you?"

"Yes, I didn't realize how lonely my existence had been. I love you Julia." I said while stealing kisses from her as well.

"What now, my love? Where are a demon and a werewolf to go in this cruel world?" Julia had said in between stealing more kisses that I returned just as quickly.

I looked at the state of my unholy garment not covering her bountiful bosoms and precious skin nearly enough. The way my shirt couldn't contain her bounty fascinated me. She was covered yet so bare all at once. I took her in my arms and flew down to the truck where I quickly placed my coat over her to conceal her sweetness from any prying eyes.

"I say we go home and have a giant bubble bath in the lagoon. First I'll stop and get us some take out." I had just said breathless from her stealing my kisses not because I needed air.

I didn't need the oxygen to survive but I needed air to just stop myself from floating into heaven from all her kisses.

"Maybe next time we'll pack some extra clothes for you." I remember smiling warmly as and devouring her with my glances as I gently placed her in the passenger seat.

I remembered us grinning at each other and then in a blink I disappeared into the woods for a few minutes. When I returned, I stopped in front of the truck to show her the three dead rabbits. She smiled and placed her index finger up to me and winked; while I smiled sweetly at her.

In another blink I dropped off those dead rabbits and had one more dead rabbit held up to show her as she blew me a kiss. Then I barely got into the truck as she rushed to my side placing one of my arms around her shoulders. She leaned against my neck and while I drove I deeply inhaled her sun-filled hair that held the sweetness of summer and the gentleness of meadow breezes of wild roses and lavender.

As I hardly held the wheel and her gently; I kept trying to stay focused on the road and not of her bare thighs. The truck had always been reliable but in this situation I wished it was a sports car; not a sturdy boat of a vehicle. *We have to make it back fast to devour those rabbits before sunset. Because we are so filthy, it's going to take hours to get clean in all the bubbles we are going to make.* I remembered thinking as my fanged smiled couldn't leave my face and my red eyes lit up like flames of hell were inside them. The old truck raced down the back roads while the dust bunnies frolicked from the kicked up dirt.

🌱🌱🌱🌱

"Thanks Dad for ending the story on that. I don't want to have to bleach my brain when I get home." Jack said and then laughed.

"Hey I toned it down. Don't let your Mom tell you our love story. Her version is wicked and she remembers it differently but just as passionately." I said as I reflected on even sweeter memories of stolen moments.

🌱🌱🌱🌱

CHAPTER 12

MIDNIGHT

I couldn't stop smiling at those memories of caring for Julia when she had been injured. I closed my eyes and could smell my wife's sweet skin over the strong maple flavored bacon. The mere scent of her made my eyes start to glow hot with a crimson fire and I couldn't stop my fangs from elongating.

"Jeeze Dad thanks for keeping it PG13 as best as you could. Can you keep those kinds of memories to yourself? Damn it, now Mom is thinking about you too. For crying out loud, telepathic connections suck. I'm just a teenager I shouldn't have to suffer through this kind of torture. I feel like barfing." Jack said as he choked on his orange juice.

"Right my Son. I love seeing memories through your Mother's eyes though. She always sees me as so handsome and brave." I said warmly as I tried to unsuccessfully retract my fangs from looking larger than normal.

"Well you know us Pendragons are extremely handsome and ferociously brave. I have to agree with her on that." Jack said and smiled sheepishly.

I looked over to my Son that had come into this world as a sweet little black wolf pup and had become this funny, charming young man before my eyes. This had happened somewhere between hikes in the woods, campfire stories, and hunting as a pack. I quickly wiped a blood tear from my eyes as I prepared a plate for the other dear human in the next cell that was stirring from the wondrous smells of the very human breakfast.

My thoughts shifted to the thick black gold wedding ring I wore. Julia and I had been married at the witching hour, up in the mountains, far from any human beings. An ancient mage gave the magical service blessed by heaven and hell. *As far as the magical world was concerned; it was forbidden for two different magical species to mingle and unite their souls for eternity. But I am in love. I am old fashioned and when you meet your soulmate you don't think; you just marry them. My heart was bewitched a long time ago; I just hadn't an idea she was the one until I found her caught in that perfect love trap. I didn't care what anyone said or what anyone thought. I knew the creatures that had created those rules were trying to stop real magic. It was the magic of true love. Those creatures that had created the rules had never experienced true love which has no boundaries, no space, and no separation of souls. All there was; was everything and it was her love. I could see her love through any darkness and even if I had to serve in hell tomorrow I would still be in heaven because of the love in my heart for her.*

Julia wore my golden ring and Jack was my Son. As far as anyone else was concerned; unless they were friendlies; they could all have their throats torn out before I would even blink in their cold direction. My deep thoughts suddenly interrupted as I noticed my watch ticking and could feel the warmth of the sun coming.

"The sun is going to rise in a couple of hours Son. You should get going so you can get some more sleep before school this morning. I just sent a message to your beautiful mother and she is waiting for you. I see you cringe but her canines aren't bared." I said warmly as I took the empty plate from my Son but gave him so more bacon for the road.

"Thanks Dad. Oh, say hello to Ollie for me. We should do another family dinner soon; make sure you ask him. I keep missing him. I'll see you before I leave for school." Jack said as he hugged me and I gave him a kiss on the cheek before he left the jail which still had prisoner in cell number three snoring in the background.

🌾🌾🌾

The dear young man in cell number three was no stranger to me and my family. I had been finding him in the gutter or under a bench for the last ten years. It was an unfortunate circumstance finding someone who was so lost and without family at such a young age.

I had become a ruler at the age of thirteen, pulling the sword from the great stone. But this individual had fallen into the pit of despair. The individual in cell number three had been a criminal and a drunk to survive almost one hard year; before I found him and took him in each night. It was a horrible thing to see someone slip through the cracks of life and he was so young when he had been orphaned.

But no Matter how much I wanted to feast on him and end his misery I couldn't. This individual was alone and maybe if he hadn't been; things would have turned out differently. But for now I listened to Ollie River snore like someone who hadn't slept in years.

Ollie River was now sobering and soon to be celebrating his twenty-third birthday as I let him sleep a few more minutes. Oliver was considered the town drunk. His golden orange curls were always seen down in the gutter. Life had been cruel to him being homeless at thirteen after losing his parents. He lived off the streets. He was a sarcastic, angry young man that everyone knew from the snide glares he gave people walking by him. He never begged for food and was always too drunk to be hungry. It was a wonder how people could give him booze and not bread. But what most people of the town didn't know; he was becoming sober and sober year after year. It had been the trauma inflicted that had wounded his heart and every day he tried he became stronger. Every person pitied him except me and I would seek him out every night; and take care of him. I would carefully keep him safe and warm in cell number three.

There were usually only two individuals that ever used the cells as a make shift hostel; and the other one was going to school in a couple of hours while this one slept like the dead. But the rest of the jail always remained empty.

🌲🌲🌲

CHAPTER 13

OLLIE HAS A WEIRD BESTIE

Ollie in his drunken demeanor had seen things over the years he wasn't supposed to see. He knew too much and he almost wondered when the supernatural being would finally finish him off and end his misery. But it seemed those days of being hunted to be slaughtered weren't coming; instead a monster had been taking care of him and feeding him before dawn each day for the last ten years. Even though the Sheriff was a slender man he always picked Ollie up with one hand effortlessly. Ollie remembered countless times of flying through the skies to the jail and being placed delicately into the bed. He even remembered the Sheriff gingerly covering him up before he slept soundly. It was always the same cell he woke up in. The jail had become his third home when he was not out in the alley; or in the abandoned wooden crate. His second home was the Sheriff's house but he never stayed there because he never wanted to be a burden. He felt like he was already a burden on society.

Ollie had awoken to the smell of bacon and eggs. As always the cell door was wide open. A place had been set at the table with a huge cup of coffee for him. It had been his custom to eat breakfast around three in the morning with the Sheriff. No Matter whom the Sheriff was eating at the time. The first time in hearing the screams and seeing the body being devoured had terrified him but he somehow became desensitized to the violence. Where normal humans would cower, he just looked on at the horrific sights over the years as just another morning. He wondered if maybe the Sheriff had done something to him to not be frightened of seeing a supernatural creature eat toes like French fries but he shrugged that thought off.

Just as the last thought escaped him he looked over to the Sheriff sitting at the table across from the plate full of delicious human food and noticed a blue human foot sans ankle attached to bulging calf cut off just below the kneecap on a turkey platter and the Sheriff smiling a huge fanged smile over to him. His eyes weren't even human; but a black onyx like shadow of where the pigment used to be and the white was completely missing like he had shiny snooker balls for eyes.

There was something definitely wrong in this unnaturally sight but at the same time Ollie was just so hungry he slowly sauntered over and sat down at the table across from his adversary or best friend; he didn't know of which was the definition of their relationship at this point because the Sheriff had a rap sheet a mile long on him.

At three in the morning they sat their eating their meals and drinking coffee. The grandest of discussions would always commence and Ollie had been learning forbidden secrets of the universe, of which he never grew tired of the wonderment of stories.

Everyone that knew of Ollie thought he was a blabbering fool, but he never paid them any mind. He was a man of the streets and he didn't care about the opinions of small minded people that had the luxuries like a permanent roof over their cleanly heads. It had been a long struggle of trying to get by during the day and being grateful he had somewhere to go at night because the Sheriff had treated him kindly. And since the Sheriff had come to finding him, this was as close to any family he was ever going to have. If it hadn't been for the Sheriff he would have died several times under the park bench or up against the corner of the dumpster where he had been beaten severely for the few dollars he had received from the Sheriff. Last night was just one of the many times the Sheriff had rescued him and eat the criminals harassing him.

But he knew the Sheriff liked messing with him, as a buddy would. The Sheriff could transform faster than he could exhale and Ollie never knew if he would have a long clawed, freakishly-monster hand pour him another cup of coffee or just an oversized human hand. But either way he was grateful for the food and to not be alone. It just took him a while to realize that this demon was a good guy.

🌱🌱🌱🌱

CHAPTER 14

MIDNIGHT

I, King Artorik Dracule Pendragon was born just and pure or else I could never have pulled Excalibur from the holy stone; but since my death and being risen there was no denying my wicked streak. Even my thirst for evil and vengeance could not be quenched. The drought that lingered in the back of my throat all day and night; needed the blood justice I gave to the wicked.

But Ollie was neither wicked nor damned. He was just lost and alone in this world. It was safe to say that I didn't actually despise Ollie at all. I had been caring for the boy since he was thirteen and genuinely wanted to be there for him.

I loved nothing better than to take care of my family and I had inavertedly adopted the young man who looked on as he creeped towards the eggs and bacon. The poor human sluggishly smiled and seemed to smell even lonelier than ever before. My black heart did care for the human but I couldn't help the darkness that loved messing with his fragile drunken reality. I was positive the human didn't quite know what had been real or what had been imagined; so I switched back and forth to my demon-vampire-bat form for shits and giggles on slow nights. But I never would go as far as to harm him and I did know when to stop taking the joke too far. I really did care too much for the lad.

Tonight was one of those slower-moving-than-the-dead nights and even though I had spent intricate care in making the scrambled eggs and the bacon just the way the lad liked; I just couldn't wait to scare my friend out of his fleshy skin. Of course the thought came across my mind that I might take it too far; but I had good notion to bring him back and gift him immortal life. But I would have to wait and see if the human's heart was up for the *pandemonium;* I would wreak on him.

In an instant my human figure was gone and my red demon eyes blazed towards the human who had just sat and looked over in horror; and then looked down at his plate. Ollie was deliciously slightly drunk and it would be fun in sobering him. The only problem was shocking him with my true-form wasn't working the way it used to and I knew something without my telepathic powers as he glanced up at me. His eyes were filled with hope as he looked at me in adoration. I had grown accustomed to our early morning ritual too. It was too bad it was going to change.

🌾🌾🌾🌾

CHAPTER 15

JACK

Jack hurried back to home sweet home. He didn't have to see his mother sitting in the kitchen having a coffee. He could just sense she was there as he took off his house key attached to a shoelace necklace. He could hear her soft footsteps coming to the door before he could even place the key in the lock.

"Son, I'm so glad you are home. Was it the rabbits again? That farmer should be arrested for tampering with Mother Nature." His Mom softly spoke but looked like she had been pacing back and forth all night.

Even as the worry spread across her face she looked simply beautiful to Jack. He loved his family; they were all good creatures of darkness. He watched as his Mother suddenly smiled at listening to his thoughts.

"Hey, no listening to my thoughts; I'm okay Mom. I fell asleep at the station again. Don't worry I was with Dad." Jack said as he grabbed an apple and polished it off his shirt before taking a huge bite.

Jack was always hungry. But there were two different variations and he was always mindful of which one. It was a life or death situation each time and he had to be careful to keep feeding the beast. He needed blood occasionally. But if that hunger wasn't fulfilled he would uncontrollably change and attack anything with a pulping vein. For now the apple was feeding him appropriately.

"I'm sorry Mom for worrying you. I'm just going to finish this apple and go back to bed before school." Jack kissed and hugged her before going down the hallway to his bedroom upstairs.

He was thankful he didn't have to sleep in the underground castle. The lagoon was cool when it wasn't being filled with bubbles or his parents. The bubbles only took a couple hours to filter out but the mental imagery of his parents scorched his brain and he hated the lagoon because of it. It was the nudity thing. Unfortunately when you grow up hunting as a pack that just happened but it was his parent's mushy love crap that Jack couldn't stand.

Jack loved his parents very much, but he was thankful he could go to school during the day when his Dad came home from his shift. He didn't have to be around the lovers. Sometimes it blew his mind how his Dad was the coolest most mucho being on the planet. He was the hero Jack wanted to be when he got older. Jack wanted to be the scary dude that ate the bad guys. And his Dad could be scarier than hell itself. After all he was a risen demon in the flesh. A natural shapeshifter of all dark creatures but his true form was more vampiric. But even as scary as his Dad was; he was a complete pushover for his Queen. His Mom had some strange power over his Dad and Jack knew neither of them would ever admit it.

In Jack's opinion his Mom was just as bad. She was always ironing his uniform and stitching it up. She was a pro at getting out blood from fabrics now. Every time his Dad requested a meal she always made it for him. She was so happy to serve her loving King.

Both were just too cute together. He just loved them with all his big swelling heart. He thought about them as he set his alarm clock and he heard their mutual thoughts back to him saying *'I love you Son'* in his mind as he drifted off to sleep. It was 4:00am and the clock was set for 7:30am. *Just great, I can get three and a half more hours of sleep; not bad for a Thursday morning.* He crashed hard but before he did he saw dancing rabbits in his dreams and seen eerie yellow eyes looking at him from the darkness of the forest shoreline, by the cool water of the quarry.

🌿🌿🌿🌿

CHAPTER 16

OLLIE

"Come on Midnight. You know that scares the shit out of me." Ollie said as he closed his eyes tightly.

"Yes I know." The Sheriff said amused at his pet name given by the locals.

He slowly retracted his elongated fangs and in the blink of an eye he was back to looking very human and boring. He gathered the newspaper he had been reading and poured more coffee into Ollie's cup for him. Ollie opened his eyes and sighed in relief at the very human looking man sitting across from him.

"I thought I heard Jack earlier. Was he okay?" Ollie said before taking a giant swig of coffee and then cleared his throat.

"Yes you heard him; he said hello and wanted to know if you could stop by for another family dinner soon. Actually, Julia and I wondered the same. It has been a month. Jack is okay, he is just having a little teenage trouble sowing his wild oats and all. He'll be fine. It's very nice of you to ask." Midnight's voice sounded eerie.

Ollie could hear the edge in the tone but wasn't concerned and continued eating as he was passed more bacon.

"So Ollie, I was speaking to the Mayor and town council and it turns out Trenton needs a gravedigger. A position just opened up. It's a steady paying job and it would keep you off the streets. Plus there is a bunkie behind St. Peters that is included as a benefit of digging for the church. It's a night shift job, so you can keep up the lifestyle you're accustomed to, including our night visits. Speak to me your thoughts out loud." Midnight said as his voice sounded a little menacing but Ollie looked at the smiling man across the table and shrugged it off.

This offer made Ollie speechless. *Are you kidding? My heart can't take this if it's a joke.* Ollie thought as he exhaled loudly and couldn't speak. No one had handed him anything. He had been struggling for so long. In fact Midnight's family and Midnight himself; were the only people that had showed him any kindness and they never stopped.

Ollie thought about how lonely he had been since Midnight found him sleeping under the park bench. It was late and it was well below freezing then. The snow and ice had burned the little exposed skin on his face. He recalled seeing his last breath escape his frozen lips when the angel came with red glowing eyes and razorblade jagged claws. The wings were so large and terrifying but he felt warmth in death's embrace. The silver star badge shone out in the darkness. He never questioned why; he just knew the Angel of Death had cared for him and gave him a warm bed in cell number three. That was ten years ago and the Angel hadn't stopped taken care of him since.

"Grave digger; ha, you never leave anything behind for me to bury!" Ollie said sarcastically and took a quick drink of his coffee as he watched a smile spread across the supernatural being's face.

"For real Midnight?" Ollie said as he choked a little on his coffee when he saw that Midnight was straight faced again.

"Yes, it's all setup. You can start tomorrow night. There is one catch though. I am your Boss. You'll be expected to have your lunch break here and visit from time to time for informal meetings, and breakfast every morning at 3:00am." Midnight said with such a straight face that Ollie was starting to feel something.

It was the feeling you get when someone was offering you a key to a new Universe and his heart started hurting because this was real. Ollie frantically swiped the few tears from his eyes and stood up so quickly walking over to the surprised supernatural Sheriff.

🌾🌾🌾🌾

CHAPTER 17

MIDNIGHT

Ollie had gotten up so fast he surprised me as he stood over my chair. I looked up but hadn't moved. I needed to control my emotions because I always needed to be stronger in any situation that life was always teaching me. Plus, I didn't want to cry in front of the human that worshipped my feet.

"So you'll have to get out of here. That cell is ready to be commissioned into an inter-office library. You won't be able to use it anymore." I stated quite frankly and watched the human shiver as he stood there.

What took me even more by surprise was that Ollie hadn't left; in fact he came closer and hugged me tight. My uniform was getting soaked from the tears Ollie was pouring out. I closed my eyes and did something against my rule of public affection; I embraced the lad back.

I had always known Ollie just needed some help to show the people of the town who he really was. Ollie was actually a hard-working, freckled face, good human; who just needed another chance.

As I stood up I embraced Ollie tighter resisting letting go until Ollie was finished crying happy tears. I thought about how the town had given permission right away but I still needed the church's permission. And the priest was a truly heartless soul. It had taken almost three years to convince the church to agree to hire Ollie as a gravedigger. I actually had to do something quite despicable to the priest. I threatened to tear off the priest's toes one by one and eat them in front of the fat bastard. I was going to enjoy it too. The priest's toes were liken to fat cherry tomatoes on a fresh garden salad.

And even in that threat; the priest remained steadfast and stubborn as a mule. I could have hypnotized him but I was looking for the compassionate way of doing things. I was hoping that the priest would open his heart and hire a poor homeless young man. But I had smelt the lie from the priest's lips when the priest said he cared for the lad but could not chance the liability of hiring a drunk. I heard his thoughts and knew it wasn't the drink to be blamed; it was about being caught doing unholy things in the church with another clergy man's wife. That loose thought from the priest pushed my patience over. I went full demon vampire on him including licking the side of his face with my long forked demon tongue. I revealed the Devil himself to the priest and told him I would wait and collect his soul by tomorrow night if he didn't hire the lad. This worked of course. Ollie was hired and the paperwork was pushed and approved by the town in ten minutes. It was a win-win. The church got livelier stating demons were among the townsfolk and Ollie wasn't homeless. Good deal for all. Besides, priests gave me bad gas and were too high in cholesterol.

I returned my focus to the young lad only five years older than Jack. What a cruel world it had been.

We both gave some manly grunts as Ollie straightened himself up and I coughed a little trying to choke back my emotions. But in all truth; Ollie had grown on me. I certainly couldn't take the thought of him falling through the cracks of life. Trenton was becoming dangerous and the evil was growing. Something big was coming. The darkness was calling me to come join the ranks. It was a feeling that never left my bones. I ignored that ill feeling and tried to be happy for my young sobering friend.

"Please sit back down and I can serve you thirds. Can I offer you some more coffee?" I smirked as the look of terror was on Ollies face once more and my elongated fangs were larger than life, in happiness of course.

With my long blue claws jagged and piercing outwards; I carefully poured the coffee into the trembling mug being held by my beloved fragile human.

🌾🌾🌾🌾

CHAPTER 18

JACK

Jack arose to the noise of his Dad getting home at 6:30am; and greeting his Mother. He quickly got up, showered and dressed to come down in time for dinner before school. They were all nocturnal creatures by nature so when his Dad got home from patrolling the graveyard shift; they would all sit down and eat dinner together as a family before Jack went to school. After school when Jack got home they would eat a huge breakfast. The family had been doing it that way ever since Jack could remember. He had no idea that humans had it backwards until he went to kindergarten. He learnt very quickly to keep these family secrets and others to himself whenever the teacher asked about his home life.

He placed his bag at the door and sat down at the table with his Mom and Dad; and they all started eating the great feast his Mother had made.

"Mmm, roast pig! Darling you outdid yourself on this dinner. It's simply to die for. And it's prepared just the way Jack and I like it. It's perfect; burnt on the outside and raw on the inside. Hey Jackie, isn't this great?" His Dad was gushing with joy while he casually used a bowing blade to slice into the meat.

Jack was still a little groggy but spoke up; "Ya, this is really special Mom. Was this the one that built his house out of straw?"

"Jack! We agreed to never speak about that anymore remember? It was only that one time and if I knew they were going to write a book; I would have had a goat for dinner." His Dad spoke in his stern voice but held a slight mischievousness in his eyes.

"Oh Son I forgot to give you this. You were holding onto it for dear life when I found you...I mean saw you." His Dad quickly recovered that little slip up as they shot quick glances at each other.

As his Dad gave him the teacup that held painted dancing rabbits Jack's head hurt. Jack couldn't remember a thing except a funny dream about the twirling bunnies.

"Hunny, what do you mean you *found* Jack?" asked Julia with a worried expression to her husband.

"My Darling I can assure you it was only kid stuff. You know these teenagers having to sow their wild oats and run with the pack." His Dad used his special soothing voice that always seemed to charm anyone and everybody.

Jack contemplated it was some kind of demon vampire charm thing and then thought to himself about how lucky he was for leaving for school in a few minutes. He looked over and his Dad gave him a quick wink. They were eating quietly and just enjoying a meal together when Jack started thinking about all the times his Dad had rescued him especially after his uncontrollable werewolf transformations throughout his childhood. *'Father' what a wonderful word I have the privilege to call the strong man beside me at the table. There's no doubt who is the Alpha; but I have never felt inferior. I have not had to crawl with my belly in the mud and grovel at his feet because he growled. Not like the other pack leader of the mining crew. I have seen that guy tear a strip off someone at the diner.* He stopped his random thoughts about his Dad only to really savor how juicy the roasted pig was. The blood oozed out the corners of his mouth and he used his tongue instead of a napkin to clean it up; not wanting to waste a single drop.

Jacks eyes went red as he started to breathe harder as his canines grew and then he exhaled loudly. In a blink his eyes turned back to the normal gray-blue they always were. Jack could feel the change that was happening but it had been subdued for a later time. That was another thing his Dad had showed him.

There were so many magical things he was taught like; bass fishing, charcoal barbequing; catching a baseball; and becoming a fierce warrior. He was taught to respect the life force in all living creatures; and that life was precious and not to be taken for granted. They hunted for blood for survival; but they never hunted for the pleasure of killing. Jack knew that side of his Dad existed; but he had never been shown that cruelty.

He looked over to his Dad and remembered how Father's day was coming up. *What do you get the man who has been on this earth for 1302 years? His life force has seen it all and had it all. What do I get my Dad to show him; he's my hero. I mean he's the whole towns hero, but he's mine first. He is also the whole town's bogeyman. I know they can feel it. I feel it too sometimes; that otherworldly evil that is in his soul. But he is my whole world. I really am lucky to have a Super Hero as a Dad. Everyone else can call him Sheriff Midnight but I get to call him Dad.* Jack's thoughts ended as he looked at his parents smiling warmly to him.

"Damn telepathy. Don't listen in anymore you guys. What if I had thought about the coolest gift? You would have spoiled the surprise." Jack said but smiled.

He wasn't fooling anyone and they all knew it. He loved them too much to even be mad about them listening to his thoughts right now. *I love you guys so much but it is cheating in regards to gift giving. You can't keep listening to my thoughts.* Jack smiled as he thought this and his Dad raised his hands up.

"Okay mister you caught me this time. I will not invasively read you conscious and subconscious mind until Father's day is over with." His deep voice sounded re-assuring.

"Okay let's shake on it." Jack said and held out his hand and his Dad grabbed it before he could get the words out.

"Slow down my dear Boy, it was just gut-instincts not reading your thoughts." Sheriff Midnight smiled warmly and they shook hands in sealing a deal with magic.

No one was reading Jack's thoughts until after Father's Day; which was in a couple of weeks. This would give Jack the perfect time to figure out what to get his glorious Dad.

CHAPTER 19

THE WITCHES DARK DEBAUCHERY

Meanwhile, in the darkest part of the forest, three witches were cackling as they sat on their overgrown mushroom stools drinking some fine toad tea. It was the finest and other magical creatures paid them handsomely in gold for the brew. They were the distribution system and co-owned the distillery. The tea itself gave prophetic dreams and could cure any ailment; except death, lycanthropy and demon vampirism. The only side effects were slight escapism from household chores and psychedelic hallucinations. The side effects were not as bad as to ever hear a complaint. Most creatures used it as a sleeping aide but the town's teenagers couldn't handle the tea and it got them higher than a rainbow Pegasus on a mountain top.

The kettle whistled loudly signaling another batch was ready. Some long bony fingers with even longer nails took the kettle off the grilled fireplace and placed it on a cozy on the table. Those same bony fingers clutched the onyx like cauldron's handle and moved it to where the kettle had once been.

"You know the Dark King slumbers. We could just chop his head off and put him back to flame. Then we could stop this plan and be done with the revolution. I just want to sit here on my arse and drink toad tea for the rest of my days anyways. I mean, why do we have to step forward? We should just let the King come and take care of his own business." The coarse voice said frustratingly.

""Hush now, Hexia. You know the light and dark of his soul. It sits in a very delicate balance; neither tipping to the light completely nor the darkness he was re-born from. I was there when we exhumed him from purgatory and I can tell you what we gave birth to that grave-yard night was not what we expected. He came back damned ten times more terrifying than we could ever imagine and more wicked than anything I have ever seen. I was fortunate to escape when I did." This witch spoke softly and looked voluptuous as she fixed her stockings very slowly.

She was teasing and tormenting the ogre that was tied to the chair across from her. She looked no more than mid-twenties but she was far older than that and only a magic mirror could show her true-leather-withered form. In this form though her skin-tight, little black dress was shockingly too short as she purposefully dropped her wand and bent over revealing her string thong to the ogre who was wide eyed.

"How dare you keep me as a lustful-prisoner to listen to this filth, Lucinda. I don't care how sexy you are. I Dufferin; am a great warrior prince and I cannot be seduced by someone older than my grandmother. So forget it Lucinda. I will not be your zombie-love-slave." Dufferin said proudly but he still watched as she slowly bent over again.

"Why does such a big strong ogre like you have to be so dumb? The word you were looking for was *'love toy'* not *'zombie-love-slave'*; and your being here is part of the plan. You will help us. I have seen it already. Not only that, you have fallen in love with me since we first met at the waterfall." Lucinda said as the other two witches were watching how uncomfortable she was making the ogre.

"I didn't know what you were back then and as I recall you kissed me." Dufferin stated but his voice cracked a little and his cheeks were an undignified pink.

"Yes, but as I recall you had no problem with kissing me back. You couldn't keep your hands to yourself and neither could I. You swore that daylight hour that you would marry me." Lucinda laughed as she placed her foot on his left muscular thigh.

"Lucinda you must have bewitched me. There would be no way that a great Prince and noble ogre such as myself, would ever fall prey to such a strange creature as you. It is forbidden for us to even be in this situation. And it was completely forbidden to be in the waterfall with you; and frolicking in the dark forest; and multiple times on the limestone cavern floor. I was disarmed then but you shall see I am no longer that weak." Dufferin let out a huge sigh as he watched while she placed her foot on his shoulder with her skirt hiked up and he continued to be in a lustful trance.

She placed her foot back on the ground and pulled her skirt down. She knew Dufferin was her soulmate. His body was a different make but he was still the same old reliable car under the hood that she had walked with through many past lives. His nature never faltered. He would pretend to resist her because of the stupid supernatural-interspecies rules and then he would fall head over feet doing all her dirty work.

"You are wrong Dufferin. I have never had to put a spell on you in any of our lifetimes together. Feel me now like you have done through the centuries." Lucinda whispered as she started kissing and sucking on his ear lobe.

Lucinda was pulling out all the tricks to break his will and make him conform. Meanwhile, Hexia gave the Old Crone a glance and the two ladies took their tea to the garden as Lucinda started slowly dancing provocative. The ogre had been rosy-cheeked before was really turning red now. Every inch of the loin clothed ogre was dripping with beads of sweat and his breathing had sped up. His muscles seemed to throb and ache in her direction.

"Now Dufferin all we have to do in push the Dark King to his full potential. He will slaughter the town and all our enemies. The humans won't have a chance. His thirst for vengeance will be un-quenchable. All we have to do is take his brain-dead Son for a couple of days and make the Dark King believe he is dead." Lucinda said as she slipped her dress over her head and that was when the ropes ripped apart.

The great ogre rushed to take Lucinda in his arms and kissed her madly; knocking over the tea pot in placing her on the table top. The sounds alarmed all the life out of the forest within a few hundred feet of the cabin. This commotion was happening while the other two witches had gone deeper into the garden. They were far away from the sounds of china and glass breaking. But both looked at each other with worrisome expressions.

"If the supreme council finds out we've been meddling with the Dark King; we will be executed this time." Hexia said as she sipped some tea.

The Old Crone sipped her tea and rolled her eyes as she looked over to the cabin in the distance.

"Forget about that. If the supreme council finds out Lucinda secretly married that ogre we are done for. But all of that is nye compared to what will happen if we don't take the Son and fuel the Dark King's rage. This is the only way. I have foreseen it in different scenarios and the end of the world will happen either way but one scenario is much more disastrous. Once the evil one comes; we are all

doomed if the Dark King continues to be a ray of loving-froggin'
sunshine." The Old Crone said and then sipped on her tea as the other
witch looked back to the farthest part of the woods near the obscure path
that led to the mountain.

🌾🌾🌾🌾

CHAPTER 20

JACK

Jack left his kissing parents of grossness and hurried off down the dirt road. His ear buds were rocking Mozart and his orange hood was up as he just made the bus. He lived so far out that he was supposed to be the last stop. The bus driver in their rebellious nature defied the normal route and went in reverse. Another oddity was the fact that even though they were all high school teenagers every student had an assigned seat. And Jacks seat was beside the new girl in town who had always wore sweat pants and hoodies. She was as mysterious as he was except he liked wearing jeans; even during track and field.

She was the new girl in town even though she had been on the bus for the last nine months. He planted his old faded blue jeans beside her pink skirt. He accidently took a second glance at her bare knees and turned away just as quickly as she caught him blushing. She was way to pretty to be a nerd like him.

He pretended to doze off to the style of catching flies. He didn't care about anything right now. He was groggy from last night. Thank the Universe they had coffee in the lunchroom. That's exactly where he was going instead of first period. It didn't Matter anyways; he was passing his classes and his final senior year of high school was almost finished.

Thump. Jack opened his eyes and seen a football on his thighs.

"Come on Jack, toss it back big boy. I know you got the pipes." The handsome blonde jock laughed deeply as Jack chuckled.

Mike Fields was his best friend and Jack knew this was a special tactic. Jack had seen this scenario many times out of Mike's extraordinary playbook to pick up ladies; and it worked. But as best friendship goes; Jack wouldn't oust him.

"Dude, you know I'm a lover not a fighter." Jack said as he casually tossed the ball up to his grinning friend that was practically hanging over the back of the seat.

"More like a snorer. I mean seriously Bro; how are you even catching zzz's at all? This bus is a zoo with hot predators on it; pretty pink skirts and all." Mike said as he winked at the pretty girl beside Jack.

Jack was momentarily lost as he saw this rosy shade spread across her cheeks. She had this sparkle to her. Jack couldn't quite put his finger on what it was. But he instantly wanted to know her.

"Well thank you Mike. I know I am pretty but don't hate me because I'm beautiful." Jack liked buttering back and forth with Mike.

He could spend every day, all day cracking jokes with his buddy. They had been best friends since kindergarten. Both were considered outsiders because their families didn't originate here. They weren't old world Trenton and that was the only kind that fit in. Even if you were born here. They both had risen out of the dirt of being a loser to star quarter back and wing man.

The only amazing and sad thing was Mike was going Pro. Mike lived and breathed football. He would practice day and night with Jack and there was never an off season. Mike had a scholarship and could finally escape this place. The only thing Jack had to look forward to was working in the mine. Jack had planned to sign up as soon as he graduated. He wanted to join the night crew and he knew he was never leaving this place.

"Well hello beautiful, my name is Mike. And this is my friend Jack who is practicing celibacy; and totally into wieners." Mike said as Jack continued to smile and blew him a kiss.

"Thanks." Jack sarcastically said and gave Mike a wink.

"My name is Azriella. You can call me Al or Ella though." She said and started to blush as Jack glanced over to her.

Jack couldn't help but notice her cheeks matching the same color as her skirt.

"I love that song." Jack said making Ella blush a deeper shade.

"Sure you do Jack." Mike was starting to sound annoyed by the deepening of his voice.

Jack knew this because of his supernatural hearing but the obvious was when he caught Mike rolling his eyes. *Holy Mike must really like the new girl. I have never seen him this frazzled by a girl talking to me before.* Jack thought as he gave a wolf-like grin to his best friend. Jack then started breathing in her floral scented perfume. The scent was triggering something familiar. She smelt like the wild roses by the quarry.

"How long have you been in town?" Jack asked and she seemed to be smirking at him now.

"Well Jack I have been sitting beside you for the last nine months." Ella spoke softly to him; as if they had been friends for centuries.

Then again his teenage hormones were raging as he smelt the intoxicating magic scent of the wild roses that only bloomed at midnight in the quarry.

"How do you like the town? There are some nice spots here…Like the forbidden ones." Mike cut in refusing to be out in round one and added some points of interest. "Did you know two kids drown in the quarry years ago? They say the woods surrounding the quarry are haunted by goblins that eat virgin teenagers. Isn't that right Jack?" Mike finished stating and smiled back just as mischievous.

Azriella was nodding with interest to Mike's story but Jack wasn't sure she really believed him. But who believes in goblins anyways? Unless you've almost fallen prey to that sweet gingerbread cottage in the deepest parts of the woods; which in this case Jack had, many times. *Thank God they didn't want to eat werewolf; it helped that I hadn't showered after gym class too.* Jack smiled at that thought while he pretended to listen to whatever Azriella and Mike were talking about.

"You know they say that Jack's dad is a demon!" Mike blurted out and Jack looked over and felt the red flash behind his eyes and then it was gone.

Jack laughed harder than normal and it was the worst of nervous laughs but everyone wasn't paying attention. All eyes and ears were only for Azriella and she seemed to be enchanting all of the students on the bus. She had literally been invisible until today when she decided to step out in the daring hot pink skirt.

Jack started feeling like an idiot in that moment. He started thinking about how many times he had seen her in hoodies and tights and not said one word to her. He had sat behind her in every one of his classes and yet this was the moment they were getting to know each other. It was when everyone else was noticing her too.

This was the first time he had not had a discussions of the weather to her. He examined the hard truth of the situation. She was showing some leg and the wolf inside was hooked on that quarry scent. It was his safe refuge and she dazzled in the scent of the magic waters. *Hmmpf. I really am a wolf.* Jack thought and tried to hide the fact that his thoughts were making him unhappy. He didn't want to be a monster he was just born that way.

"Down boy, no one says your dad is a demon. He just scares the crap out of everyone. That's all." Mike said and bent down and punched Jack in the shoulder.

The three of them started laughing.

"You kids get the hell off my bus. We've been here for the last six minutes. And if I have to wait for you little fartknockers any longer; I'm going to turn into a demon. I need a coffee right now." Yelled the bus driver.

And with that Mike, Azriella and Jack exited off the eerily empty bus. Jack really had no idea how they made it to the school so fast. And he had no idea when everyone else had gotten off the bus.

As enchanting as Ella was; Jack knew he was in trouble. He literally could lose track of time thinking about her scratching behind his ears or his backside. Hell, she could lie naked on his dead pelted-ass and he would still be enraptured by her beauty.

Right then and there he made up his mind to avoid Ella at all costs. He would be completely dis-interested in everything about her. He was lonely but he had goals. He was determined to join the pack. He wanted to run with the wolves and eventually become an Alpha. But she was going to screw it all up. So back to the shadows he would go. Forget love; it was for suckers and the dreamless. And he was a lone wolf.

🌲🌲🌲🌲

In gym class they were playing dodgeball and Jack was tired and hungry. He was going to make everyone around him pay. Except the ladies of course; he'd still get them out but tap them gently with the ball.

His new philosophy was if he was going to have to be alone for the rest of his life; so did everyone. They all had to be out too. He grinned as he caught the first ball and threw it hard. It rebounded off some poor guy's belly. *That guy's going to see the nurse today. Lucky Jerk; ya, you can thank me later dude.* Jack thought as he smiled wickedly throwing the ball hard at Mike and nailing him in his butt.

It is to mention that Jack didn't want to seriously injury people. He was just a little hormonal because of the after effects of the full moon and missing his morning coffee.

It is also good to mention some much needed information about the nurse. She wasn't just anyone. The nurse used to be the bikini cover girl spokeswoman for this worldwide popular beer franchise called; *"Wowzers"*. She had modelled her way through University. Even though she was a certified nurse and in her late thirties; she could stop traffic with her glamour. There wasn't any man in the school and in the town that didn't want to be sick and visit Lucinda the nurse legitimately.

🌾🌾🌾

CHAPTER 21

OLLIE

Even before the alarm went off Ollie was listening to the soft rain on the tin roof of his new bunkie. He was finally home. This was the first time in ten years that he had a bed that was all his. There would be no more frozen park benches with newspapers as blankets for Ollie ever again. This was his new paradise and had taken over the proceeding jail cell which the Sheriff had taken up for him. The small cabin had one room with a small table and two chairs; and three windows. He had a beautiful view of the river, the cemetery, and the woods. He had cupboards with food and a small kitchenette area.

There was a small bathroom off the main room; and this space had been renovated to the max as a gift from Midnight. This was everything he had ever wanted in a place and it came without bars. It was his hope and promise of a better life. And this morning was the very beginning of all the wonderful things to come with second chances.

He sat up and gently moved the thick quilt off him as he stretched. This was such a lovely wooden cottage that he couldn't even believe it was all his. He wiped a few tears from his eyes as his heart swelled at what the Sheriff had done for him. No one in the town cared for him except the demon. Everyone only thought of him as a drunk and he knew it. But no one had given him food except the Sheriff. Everyone would pass him alcohol and on his empty belly of course his senses would be off.

"I'm going to be somebody now. I have a good job and I am going to keep it forever." Ollie spoke into the darkness but was dead sober as he wiped more tears.

"I can do it world, despite what you think. I am more." Ollie shouted and wiped more tears as he got up.

The floors were warm from the thermo-heated tiles and he wriggled his toes on the smooth stone. *Things are going to be different now. I can feel it. Thank you God for my best friend Midnight; I don't know what I would have done without him all those years ago. Thank you for renovating the space for me Midnight.* Ollie prayed as he thought about when his parents had died and the demon that had found him after six months of being on the streets with no help. He looked now out his window at the being with glowing eyes frantically digging a grave open. He watched the kind creature with great leathery wings feeding off the newly buried librarian. *That is my answered prayer.* Ollie thought as he winced at his Boss ripping off a thigh like a drumstick and biting into the thick blue flesh of that thick bountiful lady.

Ollie continued to watch as he made himself a coffee while those glowing red eyes watched him while it fed. *She must have been quite tasty. I never saw him feed so viciously before. He must have been starving.* Ollie thought as he turned from the scene to get his clothes on.

His thoughts drifted to the young teen he was when Midnight had found him. *It had been such a crazy life being orphaned at thirteen; but then amazingly found and practically adopted by the town's bogeyman.* He closed his eyes and could remember passing out in the cold. He remembered being carried by the strong cold arms of death. Those strong arms had placed him lovingly in a bed and covered him with many blankets. It was that same demon that had fed him soup when he was sick; and then fed him scrambled eggs and bacon at three in the morning each night thereafter. The demon would scare him and cook him breakfast. But always took care of him. That was the way of their friendship.

He closed his eyes remembering all the times Midnight had taken him fishing in the dark. They sat in a little row boat in the darkness with little bells on their lines and seashell bras as bait tied to a hook-less line. He couldn't even remember how many mermaids they had caught, kissed and released. There were so many magical memories as he got older and began to be less and less afraid; and drank less and less alcohol.

Ollie also clearly remembered that day he was at the graveyard visiting his parents and in earshot of the quarrel Midnight was having with the priest. Ollie didn't like ease dropping but couldn't resist listening at the commotion and he covered his mouth to squash the scream that he fought to swallow when he saw the Sheriff turn into the demon in broad daylight. He knew what they had discussed and this incident had confirmed that Midnight truly was the only one in the whole world that was always looking out for him.

He couldn't believe how far he had come. He was super excited at the thought of finally being able to do something with his life. Tonight he turned twenty three in his own place. *Life doesn't get any better than this.* Ollie thought as he started pulling on his boots when the door magically opened.

The gruesome figure hovered just before the door but had not stepped his clawed-foot inside. The giant leathery wings barley flapped as the red eyes watched him struggle with the bootlaces.

"Please come in and out from the cold, my friend." Ollie said as he looked up but put his head down to struggle with the double knots he had tied so tight they were impossible to untie.

The blue-black gangly hand reached to the boots laces and magically loosened them and then gingerly tied the boots in perfect bows for Ollie. As he looked up in thanks his breath still escaped him every now and then; when he looked at the demon smiling warmly to him. Everything always seemed so surreal. But he knew Midnight would never harm him. Even with those incredibly long and sharp fangs that seemed to grow when Midnight was hungry or happy.

Tonight was just another night of their weird friendship of which his heart sang for. That was his held secret. He never told anyone. Not even to Midnight himself would he ever tell him how much the demon vampire actually meant to him.

The great demon vampire didn't say a word but placed its large hand behind its back and then brought it forth holding a small chocolate cupcake with icing and a lit candle. And then in the most disturbing supernatural voice ever heard by a human said; "Happy Birthday Oliver. Make a wish."

Ollie grunted as he couldn't stop the tears that crept out of his big eyes. *He remembered. He always remembers. What an amazing thing my life has been so far. What a privilege to be in the presence of the last true King on this earth and friends with a Guardian Angel.* Ollie thought as he looked at the considerate cupcake and then the blood still hanging off the fangs of his friend. *What an amazing life. I wish to always have my best friend in my life even in the hereafter.* Ollie's happy thoughts were bursting with love as he made his wish.

Ollie took a huge breath and blew out the candle in one blow;

keeping his eyes closed in making his true heart of heart's wish.

CHAPTER 22

MIDNIGHT

I knew my eyes looked bright red and evil but they were a deception as I listened to the human's secret wish. I exhaled in a breathless sigh as the human was completely bursting with happiness and love. I felt the same way. Ollie was this little snot-nosed kid that I couldn't help but care for all of these years. Life had been cruel to the penniless human and even though it has always been forbidden to intervene with mankind. I would be damned if I just stood by while the kid died. And that was how I became the human's father figure and friend.

Even now as I watched the human offer me some of the cupcake and his only birthday cake; I was star-struck at the generosity of someone who had nothing. *Yes, my child and that is why I chose you too. I wish you didn't have to work on your birthday but it was the deal I made with that wicked priest in order to board you here.* I thought and declined the piece of cupcake offered and instead grabbed the shovel for my friend.

I opened my arms and Ollie moved into them for a hug while we flew out into the darkness of the graveyard. We had flown past the church and garden of remembrance; over six acres of land. We were going to the new fields of fresh grave sites in the very back of the church's consecrated earth.

I gently landed and my feet felt the heat, emitting a slight smoke from touching the holy ground. *In the good old days I would have caught fire but I am beyond that death now.* I chuckled to myself as I watched Ollie walk over to the two marked spot's which held the small rope frame.

While Ollie started to dig I went over to my current snack of Ms. Merriweather. She had been such a grand feast and I couldn't resist the taste of her flesh. She had an old books scent off her skin like she had lived and breathed for the volumes of history at her lifelong profession. I couldn't help it as I licked my fingers after ripping another piece of thigh off her corpse. She was so addictive and I was eating more vulgar than I had ever dared in front of the human. I had been famished and craved the old librarian's flesh like a junk food addict. There was just something about her that I couldn't get enough of. If I had to, I would have sold my soul to eat her corpse before it rotted completely. And even when she had rotted completely I still would have ripped the coffin lid off to eat her corpse. *Ms. Merriweather is simply too delicious for me to let rot.*

Ms. Merriweather was only a couple of days old, freshly dead from old age and in a peaceful sleep. I had threatened the mortician not to touch her body or else there would be two in the casket. Although Ms. Merriweather had been friendly enough to the town; the service had been short with few in attendance and I had been fortunate to exhume the body that night. She was a sensation of delights that I wanted to share with my wife. But Julia didn't appreciate the hint of flavors of old russian cigars and decrepit mothballs like I did.

It had been a dreadful thing of dismembering her just enough to fit into the casket but it was the only way I could get the lid closed for the show. The funeral was thirty minutes before sundown and everyone including the priest was long gone when the dirt lightly covered the wooden dripping box. She had been that fresh; and I could barely contain myself as I secretly commanded everyone except Ollie to leave so I could dig her up and rip off the lid.

I also took pleasure in Ollie looking at me through eyes filled with gratitude instead of disgust as I really took huge chunks off Ms. Merriweather's meat. *My human is watching but not turning away this time. I just can't help myself she has this sweet buttery taste with a hint of garlic. There is a hint of disgusting boiled onions but other than that she is flagrantly full of donuts and honey-barbeque chicken. That's it; she has bested me in her death. This is from that sweet honey-barbeque chicken recipe that she took to her grave even when I pleaded with her. God I hope she likes rotting in hell. No, I must not condemn her. But damn she tastes so good. The more I eat of her, the more I might learn the secrets of her recipe. Take that Ms. Merriweather. Feel my vengeance as I crunch your bones for not giving me the recipe at the town Strawberry Social.* My thoughts were horribly delightful as I changed focus to the tangy sweet flavor of Ms. Merriweather's full hairy armpits. I let out a horribly exotic roar full of the glee from ripping and chewing more of her flesh.

⚜⚜⚜⚜

"Okay Oliver, we have two graves tonight to dig and then the re-burying of that no-good witch, Ms. Merriweather. It just rained so the ground will be heavy but soft to cut into. Unlike Ms. Merriweather's thick two-ton bag of flesh. She was a tough old bird but aged to perfection and sizzled in sin." I could hear my grizzly voice being uplifted as all kinds of fluids dripped down my dimpled chin.

"No problem Boss. I'm on it. You can count on me." Ollie sounded cheerful and started singing while shoveling dirt.

I flexed my wings as I looked a little suspiciously over to Ollie.

"I mean; for crying out loud Midnight. You just ate Ms. Merriweather of all people? You probably just raised your cholesterol a whole other supernatural level. Was she worth it?" Ollie spat out with a wolfish grin and I chuckled.

Then I let out the most unholy belch in existence of the creation of the earth; panicking the nearby vultures waiting for any dropped morsels. Ollie giggled at how frightened the birds were when they took off.

"Good ole' Ollie, never change my friend. I have to leave you now and head into town because I am needed. And you have to pretend not to be too happy or the priest will definitely kick you out. I shall see you at three." My voice was menacing but my smile was heartfelt.

I hoped that my human felt the warmth over the darkness in my voice. I carefully placed the casket lid back on the wooden box and then gently hovered with my leathery wings flapping towards the gloomy vultures. The wind from my wings deliberately blew the dirt back over Ms. Merriweather's open grave, filling the hole completely for my friend.

I looked back as I watched my human smiling while he was working. Then I watched as my human tried to hide his smile. *My dear friend, have this night of merriment and we shall see each other again for breakfast.* I thought and then groaned at having to put back on my uniform and rescue the cat that was stuck in the dreaded tree again.

Ms. Merriweather was finished and her coffin was re-buried. So I really had to answer the call from the station. I could hear Doris tapping her long manicured red nails on the desk impatiently. Doris was the receptionist and a semi-retired hybrid-dragon. I didn't want to catch fire in making her wait; even though most nights I felt it would be easier to just eat that damn cat that always got stuck in the tree. *Thank God Merlin the kitten wasn't like that or I probably would have eaten him. Such a long time ago when that little fluff ball came into my life. I'm so glad I made him a hell cat to keep him for all of eternity.* My thoughts wandered as I paused and watched Ollie's happiness never falter. *I didn't want to worry my human but I didn't know how to tell him I accidently spilt my blood into his cupcake batter. I was stirring with my switchblade and got distracted as my thumb hung over the bowl. I think I'll save this information for another time. Besides he doesn't have to worry unless he passes away within the next week and that's not going to happen with me as a guard dog watching over him.* My thoughts wandered but I knew I had to leave. Seeing Ollie so happy was just as intoxicating as eating Ms. Merriweather. My heart felt full of pride at seeing the young man he was becoming; he was far removed from the lost boy he used to be.

So instead of leaving, I just hovered across from my adopted human; watching and listening to his happy thoughts. I felt like everything was right in the world and my dear one had finally found his place in this dimension of his existence.

🌿🌿🌿🌿

CHAPTER 23

THE FARMER'S SECRET

The flies were biting in the hot summery night and the rotting meat turned a perfect flavor of foulness. He greedily grabbed more meat steamed from the sun. The figure dabbed his mouth as the dead tissue left remnants on the corners of his perfect red lips. The salty tissue reminded him of the blubbery fat off the sides of bacon and he moaned as the piece of flesh slid down his throat.

He took another fatty slimy piece of meat and sucked on the juices before chewing and swallowing it slowly. *Heaven. I am in Heaven once again seated next to the beast. There is so much of this human that I can be living happy for days if I wished for leftovers. If this human goes undetected any longer, his fat ass will be gone by tomorrow at the rate I'm consuming him. But I am being rather silly. As great as an adversary as King Artorik is, even his supernatural abilities haven't detected my superb acting skills; and it has been months of this charade.*

Then again, I did steal Guinevere out from under his big nose when I was human. He had no idea I was a cannibal even in all the crusades we fought together. Her flesh was something so fragrant too. I haven't tasted the likes in years. Why should I save anything for later? I deserve fresh meat. I deserve those mortals unconditional love and to be worshipped. The humans should plead to be re-born into servitude for their new King. Who does Pendragon think he is anyways? I never made him my King. I never took a bended knee in Avalon or Camelot; no Matter what the Lady of the Lake had said. She was a fool for nurturing my ambitions and tasted my blade along with Guinevere. I was raised from the grave too King Artorik and I shall best ye in battle like the dual that we should have had long ago. I gave all the secrets to the Ottoman Empire to kill you and they still couldn't. It has been centuries of tracking you down and now we are finally here in this shithole of a town. The shadowy figure's thoughts were nasty like the meat he just finished eating. He jumped in the shower and started washing the dirt off his skin while looking outside the window at all the giant rabbits in the field. Every now and then you would hear a bear trap go off and it made him smile like some sweet medley of metal and screaming.

"Who would have thought the great battle for the world would end up in Canada? Sure as hell not me, I would have rather it be in Las Vegas where you can smell the sin off the streets. Why is the gateway to hell always in the dullest of places? Tell me rabbits or die." The dark figure bellowed as all the rabbits scattered from the voice calling out to them from the bathroom window.

"Fine don't tell me you little shitheads, I'll be eating you later. I have to get ready for my night out with the horny bingo hall ladies." The deep voice oozed with supernatural male bravado as they arrogantly laughed while watching themselves dress in the mirror.

"I'm not much to look at when it comes to muscles but at least I'm hung like a horse. Let's see if this middle-aged man can still make all the bingo ladies rancid with desire." His voice lightened as he practiced in the mirror talking in the voice of the body he had taken.

"Yes, this cologne shall do nicely I think. Damn, I need the straw hat. My pointed ears will give me away and maybe my fangs. Aw hell, those ladies won't be looking at my ears or teeth." His voice sounded more and more human as he pulled up his suspenders and chuckled.

His cotton-collared shirt and jeans weren't as dashing as his old suit of armor but he felt like gold; all shiny and valuable. He couldn't stop admiring how tasty he looked in his new skin but he dragged himself away from the mirror as the clock started chiming five times.

"King Artorik is going to pay and I will make him suffer. Do you hear me you oversized stuffed animals? I don't care what the prophesy says. I am winning this fight and he can go straight to the underworld as a coward. I will be the General and lead the armies to conquer the world. And then I will take his new bride and taste her delicious heart too." The figure shouted in the mirror as he looked at the reflection of the rabbits in the field now watching him again through the large living room window.

The rodents' black beady eyes were all over him and he suddenly felt a shiver go down his spine. He quickly looked over to the pile of dirt and then to the large gathering of rabbits with their ears perked and all eyes locked on him. *I re-buried him deep. They couldn't possibly want that much revenge on this human can they?* His thoughts stopped mid-sentence as he swore all the rabbits just nodded their heads in a *yes* to him. Then he seen the unnatural look they had all given him. He knew the look because it was the way he always looked at his next meal.

He left the window of unwanted attention and made his way to the foyer. *Screw those rabbits. I can get more bear traps if they want to play that game. Or I can just shapeshift to a bear and eat them all.*

That's a good plan for after I take over the world. As long as they don't dig up the man that terrorized them for so long, everything will work out just fine. He thought as he looked at the hallway mirror and straightened up his bow tie.

He straightened his hair again as he thought about how his night was going to go and tried to calm down his large excitement. *I can't wait to take Hexia again. I have my handkerchief this time. She's so annoying when she screams. I'm going to enjoy bending her over the sink and making her bleed.* His fangs had elongated at that last thought and he had a hard time retracted them. So he focused on adding more cologne to his thick neck. But he knew he didn't need it. The pheromones he was emitting could seduce a nun.

He knew as he flashed his handsome grin that those ladies at the bingo hall wouldn't know what would come over them. He was going to give them all hot flashes and then he was going to give them all the very best passionate-time of their abruptly shortened lives.

He knew the Sheriff would be pre-occupied with that stupid cat in the tree he magically placed there again. Tonight was his and nothing could stop him from having fun with all the ladies. *Rivers of blood are going to flow tonight. I'm going gorge myself on all the cougar's love in the bingo hall. I love being so damn hot; I'm almost too good to be true. For all the prayers I'm going to falsely answer tonight; hell should be giving me extra points.*

※※※

CHAPTER 24

JACK

Arrangements had been made pretty quickly and everyone was meeting up tonight for a mixer at the quarry. It had been a long time since everyone had snuck out and had a little fun. Jack took off another shirt and threw it on his bed as he tried to figure out what perfect shirt would make him seem cooler to a certain pretty green eyed girl.

The summer was hot and they would all end up swimming later but he still wanted everything to be perfect. He had even picked a couple of roses for her and bled for her in doing so. *I can't believe another month has gone by and my plan of avoiding Azriella has been failing. She sits near me in every class and we've even been paired up in drama classes. I just feel like an idiot when I'm alone with her. But I still have this feeling like I know her. There's just something I can't explain about her.* Jack's thoughts were anxious and loud as he paced back and forth in his room.

The full moon had just past but he was still feeling a little moody.

The creak on his front step and the knock at his front door took him a little by surprise as he changed his shirt one more time before spritzing himself with more cologne and running out of his room.

"I'll get it." Jack yelled as he knew his Mom was going for it and beat her just in time.

He took a big breath and opened the door.

"Hi Jack, I hope I'm not too early. You did say we could go together right?" Azriella said and blushed as Jack's mouth dropped open in seeing her in a hot pink bikini string top.

This was the most skin he had ever seen on Azriella. She looked like a movie star dream in a micro-mini skirt with platform sandals and a beach bag. *Is it possible for Azriella to be getting even prettier?* She had on these posh sunglasses and silver hoop earrings and looked glamourous. And Jack was almost at a loss for words.

"Ah, ya...I mean yes. Of course, please come in. I just need to brush my teeth and then we can leave." Jack stammered out and then ran back to the bathroom.

While he was brushing his teeth he strained to hear his worst nightmare proceeding in the living room. His Mother had introduced herself and proceeded to show Azriella embarrassing baby photos; and then adolescent photos of him in a speedo swimming at the quarry. They were talking about how much Jack had loved hiking and how cute Jack looked eating spaghetti. Of course this was all true. But then he heard the; *"you can go and make yourself at home; Jacks room is on the left."* And at that moment he remembered the careless items of his jock strap and clothes strewn about. He also remembered his baby stuffy of a vampire doll on his bed, which his Dad gave him and he still slept with. His toothbrush dropped out of his mouth as he could hear her footsteps by his dresser and smelt her spray his cologne.

His heart started racing. *Is she curious or does she like me too?* He grabbed his toothbrush and rinsed it off and left the bathroom to walk in on her holding his vampire stuffy and smelling it.

"That's just some doll my Dad gave me as a joke." Jack said as she squeezed it in a hug and unapologetically smelt it again.

"The smell of this doll is just so comforting. I don't know what it is Jack. Reminds me of a flower but I just can't place my finger on the scent. So, what was the joke? And what's with this teacup on your dresser? My grandma owns the same tea cup set which is really weird." Azriella said as Jack reached over and gently took the doll from her and placed it on his dresser.

"Oh ah, we should get going. Mike is going to meet us down the road and it's a bit of a walk into the quarry. I have my backpack ready full of bug spray, marshmallows, coolers, sunblock, and my towel." Jack said changing the subject.

"Oh, I need sunblock. I burn easily. Do you think you could help me out and put some on my back?" Azriella said as she turned from him and dropped her beach bag and towel.

She threw her sunglasses on the bed and lifted her hair bending over slightly for him. He could see her watching him in his mirror. It was the same old mirror on his dresser but suddenly she made it seem exotic as it had never seen a beautiful woman before. He took out the sunblock and tried not to shake as he fumbled the container. He took the quietest big breath of his life as he squeezed some lotion on her back. This was one of those fantasies he had always wanted to live out but somehow in real life the moment seemed more precarious.

When he started rubbing the back of her neck he hadn't even noticed the strings loosening with each movement of her arms and the slight tilting of her head. But his values were strong even as a wolf he was always a gentleman first. When her strings came loose and her top fell off; he moved supernaturally fast in grabbing the towel to cover her.

"Oh my heavens." Azriella said looking more embarrassed then sexy and Jack blushed as he wrapped her before she could say another word.

They stood facing each other for a moment as he saw the tears filling up her eyes and her hands stayed over his; as he held the towel up for her. He paused for another moment to find the right words and show her he wasn't some kind of monster. *Sheesh that was close. Man, I hope she doesn't say a word about how fast I moved just now. Oh no, I don't think I can take her crying. My heart will break if she doesn't stop; and then I'm gonna start.*

"One time Mike and I were at the pool in school and we were play-fighting. He accidently pulled down my shorts in front of the whole gym class and I thought I was going to die right then and there. And now there are never ending jokes. But as mortifying as that was; I still go to class and hold my head high. At least this happened here in the presence of a friend and not around everyone." Jack said as he stayed holding the towel and she continued holding his hands too.

"You are so right. I'm really sorry Jack. I wanted to look pretty for the party but this wasn't on purpose. I'm so glad I have you for a friend. You saved the night. You are my hero." Azriella said as he wiped the tears from her eyes.

"Can you please help me do it up again?" Azriella said as she turned away from him and fixed her top with the towel still being held up by Jack.

She carefully passed the two strings back. Jack let the towel drop to the floor and it seemed to echo off the wood. He quickly grabbed the strings and gently tied them in a tight perfect bow; both sections.

"There it's tied in a double knot this time. You can swim without worry tonight." Jack whispered as she turned around and hugged him.

"Thank you again; I don't know what I would do without a good friend like you." She said so warmly and kissed him on the cheek but Jack was instantly depressed.

He knew what this meant. *Oh no. I'm friend-zoned. I wonder if she likes Mike more than me? I am moody and sometimes I have death breath from whatever I ate. I didn't know my heart could be this happy and hurt this much at the same time. Aw, who am I fooling? Who could love a creature of the night?* As Jack thought the worst he faked a sneeze so he could wipe the little tears from his eyes and still reclaim his dignity.

"Oh, bless you." She softly said as he blushed when her eyes stayed for a moment longer looking into his.

"Thanks sorry about that. I get allergies. We should get going I'm just going to grab my sweater."

"Do you really think you need it? It's so hot out."

"Well you never know by the quarry, sometimes the north wind blows down from the mountain just to ruin teenagers having fun. It's like the curse of this town." Jack laughed and stuffed his hoodie in his backpack and sprayed himself with some more cologne.

He grabbed his baseball cap and casually kicked his jock strap under his bed hoping she hadn't seen it, even though it was on the floor in front of the dresser. *Kill me now. Uuugghh; I hope she wasn't looking at my jockstrap this whole time.*

"Ready my lady?" Jack sounded a little happier as they were finally leaving his room and she followed him out.

"Mom we are just going to the quarry I'll see you around eleven." Jack called out but his Mom grabbed his hand and pulled him into a quick hug.

"Okay, keep safe baby boy, love you." Julia said as Jack kissed her cheek goodbye.

Jack and Azriella waved goodbye and then hit the road towards the quarry. Azriella looked like some movie star again as her shades flashed a little in the sunlight.

"You know you have a very cool Mom. I like her a lot." Azriella said.

"Yes, she is pretty cool. She knows I'm pretty responsible so she trusts me." Jack said as he offered to take Azriella's towel and beach bag for her; and she happily let him carry her stuff.

"My Mom passed away last year but it has been okay. I didn't know her very much. My grandma raised me. She's been pretty strict but tonight she said I could sleep over at Selena's house if it gets too late and I didn't want to walk alone." Azriella said and looked across a field.

"Oh I wouldn't let you walk alone. Neither would Mike; we make sure everyone gets home safe always." Jack said but noticed she still wasn't looking at him.

Azriella switched topics to talking about poetry. And Jack was listening to her but couldn't stop looking at how the sunlight was making her hair have golden streaks throughout the curled tresses. *I could listen to her voice forever and never be tired of hearing her pitches and tones. If I didn't know better I would swear she was part mermaid.*

"Hey losers, I knew you missed me. Damn Ella, you look finer than the steak I ate for dinner and I had a large, T-Bone. You know speaking of which...Has Jack ever told you why we nicknamed him *Horse?*" Mike snorted.

"Okay that's enough Mike, Ella does not want to know. Let's talk about your top picks for scholarship's and which universities you got fighting over you." Jack said and changed the subject but caught Azriella looking at him with a raised eyebrow.

That changed the subject perfectly though and took the heat off him. Mike loved nothing better than to talk about football and winning over the scouts at the last game. Mike cracked a beer and passed them each one as they continued to walk down the dirt road.

⚜⚜⚜⚜

A nice little campfire and some music and all seemed right in the world. They went from ghost stories and roasting marshmallows to swimming in the quarry with only the fire and some tiki torches as their light. It was a beautiful Friday summer night, even though it was the second week in June. The water was refreshing as the air grew hot instead of cooling down as the night went on.

They started playing Marco Polo and Jack was hiding against the rock with Azriella plastered against his chest as she closed her eyes. Mike was dangerously close to them and Jack could feel her heartbeat still racing as they both tried to hold their breath.

"Marco." Mike called out

"Polo." Everyone shouted together and really startled Mike.

Mike suddenly changed directions as if hearing his prey and swam almost to the shore and far away from Jack and Azriella. Mike was almost catching Steven as Jack looked over at the commotion. When he stopped holding his breath he looked down and into the green eyes that were looking into his. He just realized he had been hugging Ella tight and she was still hugging him back even though Mike was going to catch Steven in two more steps. She looked up and closed her eyes and Jack bent down feeling her breath on his lips almost touching the smoothness.

"Hey you guys Steven's it." Mike shouted and startled everyone just before Jack could kiss her.

Mike had been so loud his voice frightened everyone and everyone quickly moved away from each other as he splashed forward. Jack's heart hurt at the almost encounter. Azriella's skin was so soft in Jack's arms and all he wanted to do was have his first kiss. And he wanted it to be with her. *Maybe it just isn't meant to be. I think though, I could be happy with us being friends for the rest of my life. I guess.* Jack thought as she suddenly grabbed his hand trying to save him by hiding with her. He found himself completely happy, holding her again as they hid against some flat rocks. *She's holding me back. Maybe she does like me?* Jack thought as he closed his eyes and she hugged him tighter.

🌿🌿🌿🌿

The group climbed out of the water and went back to the campfire to dry off and tell more monster stories. Almost all the ghost stories were about Jack's Dad but he didn't care. To Jack, his Dad was his hero even though everyone saw him as a villain. Mike was always the first one to speak about Jack's Dad like he knew all of their family secrets.

"One time I swear I saw Midnight Demon stand on the hood of his patrol truck and made the truck drive. He's that magical." Mike said and laughed.

"Ya right Mike." Jack said and chuckled.

"No it's true. I saw it too. I also have seen his eyes go blood red." Steven piped in.

"I think Sheriff Midnight is dreamy. He easily has to be the best looking person in the town. He should have gone in to acting. He's that hot. But in a spooky kind of way." Selena giggled and winked at Jack.

Mike just rolled his eyes.

"Folks my Dad is just a cool guy that busts bad dudes that's it." Jack said and laughed.

"I have seen him flying one time." Azriella piped in and everyone stopped laughing and looked at her seriously.

"He flew right into my bedroom window and into my dreams."

Azriella said and then everyone laughed.

Jack mouthed the words to her *'you too?'* and she shrugged and continued laughing with everyone. Then an Old Crone in a black dress came out of the forest suddenly and everyone gasped. She looked like she could raise the dead as her mean eyes scanned the crowd.

"Mike here is the two jugs of toad tea you ordered and the pizzas. That will be sixty gold doubloons. Everyone here is eighteen right? I will know if there are minors drinking and I will report them to the Sheriff." The Old Crone cackled but everyone knew she wasn't joking.

"Yes. There is no one here that is a minor. Jack do you have any money?" Mike said and Jack rolled his eyes.

"Yes, I got it." Jack said and came over to where the woman was standing and Mike grabbed the pizza boxes and the liquid potion.

"You only need a couple of drops in each beer. Any more and the secrets will start to come out; including things you want to remain hidden. No one will remember in the morning but no more than a few drops. A word of caution; there is some foulness a foot in town stay together and all will be well." The Old Crone cackled as Jack passed her the pirate's gold and a giant ruby as a tip.

Then a puff of sparkly smoke appeared and she was suddenly gone but everyone heard her car start and the tires squeal away.

"You heard the lady; all night sleepover at the quarry. Yippee." Mike said and everyone cheered as they started eating.

Mike started pouring a lot of the tea in everyone's open cups.

"Wait Mike, that's too much. This is powerful stuff; remember what happened the last time?" Jack said as he rushed over to his friend giving Azriella way too much.

"What are you chicken? Besides the only thing I remember from the last time was us wrestling and I winning the match in showing off your prized horse." Mike laughed as he held the whole bottle up to

Jack's face.

Jack put his hands up to push the bottle away.

"I dare you to drink this whole two litre bottle so we can have some supernatural fun. Don't worry I am drinking a lot too, my pack brother." Mike said as his eyes flashed yellow only to Jack.

"We can't be free. We can't be ourselves. What if the humans remember our differences this time and the magic we hold?" Jack whispered to Mike.

"With how much we are drinking tonight. No one is going to remember anything. Besides they already know and want to be like us." Mike whispered back.

"Come on chicken. Boc boc buc boc; Jack is a chicken. Jack is a coward. Look even Azriella drank her whole cup. Besides we still have half a jug left; even if you crack open this new bottle and devour it. Don't be a wimp. Let's go Jack." Mike shouted and everyone started calling Jack's name over and over.

"Fine. But we aren't going into town this time and eating anyone. I mean it." Jack shouted and then tilted his head and drank the whole two litre bottle of magic toad tea.

Mike hooted and cheered him on as everyone lifted their glasses and drank as fast as they could.

"Let the games begin. We can see everyone's magic-self now." Mike shouted and laughed as two other kids bent over immediately while glowing.

The toad tea was a magic potion that not only got everyone drunk it transformed you to your true-form; and the teenagers of the town had been experimenting with it for years as it gave them a rush. The only bummer was the incredibly bad hangover the next day.

Jack made sure he stood behind a tree to hide as he discarded his shorts and T-shirt. He didn't want to rip through them and he started glowing. Even though he tried to hide as well as some of the other teens who were almost howling in pain; Azriella chased after him. And he couldn't stop the change as he watched her discard her garments and transform with him. They were standing there wide eyed watching each other. It occurred to Jack at this moment Azriella had never seen a werewolf. But then Jack had never seen a fairy before as her wings pierced through the skin on her back. And immediately he heard her thoughts of never transforming in front of anyone before. He was her first.

Her wings were iridescent in the moonlight; and she had all these strange markings of ivy and flower tattoos all over her body. She had fiery red hair and even brighter yellow eyes that glowed. Her skin was this pale green and she had this dark green vine with leaves that seemed to cover her indiscretions like some nature bikini. *She's a fairy. Azriella is supernatural like me. She's beautiful.* Jack thought as he howled.

When everyone returned to the fire there was; three werewolves; three flower nymphs; three centaurs and one fae. Out of twenty teens half were magical. But Jack was the largest werewolf out of everyone and his red glowing eyes couldn't contain his happiness as they glowed even brighter.

Someone turned back on the radio cranking the volume and everyone started dancing. Selena started twirling with Mike and to the average person; a human dancing with a werewolf would be strange but not tonight. The humans and the supernatural beings were friends even with their obvious differences; and tonight was just another night of magical fun and mischief.

They decided to play another round of Marco-Polo and Azriella became it. It was obvious as she made her way through the screaming teens she was on a mission and tracked Jack down. He was in a run and just made it to the shore as she tackled him. Then she assaulted him with tickling and sweet kisses all over his laughing face.

"Okay I'm it. It's my turn and this time if I catch you I get to bite you and turn you into a werewolf." Jack shouted and everyone screamed and took off into the water giggling.

"Bite me first Jack." Steven said as he giggled and mooned Jack before running into the water.

"You'll have to wait your turn Steven; I have a fairy in my sights." Jack said feeling like he finally had the liquid courage to kiss Azriella back; if only he didn't have to be blind folded for the game.

"Hey big guy cover up those red eyes with your handkerchief." Mike said as his voice was almost a growl.

Mike was a gray werewolf with yellow eyes and Selena held his hand as they ran into the water away from Jack. Azriella winked at Jack before she ran away from him too. *Oh I'm gonna enjoy catching the humans tonight and one lovely fairy. Actually, I hope I only catch the fairy.* Jack thought as he couldn't lose his grin while covering his eyes up.

"I'm coming to get everyone. Marco." Jack said as his voice sounded menacing.

"Polo." Everyone shouted as they all tried to squash and snuff out giggles as the giant werewolf moved into the water coming for them all.

A dark figure in the tree line with red eyes had watched the commotion and secretly placed a protection spell over the frolicking teenagers trying to have fun in a world that sometimes refused to acknowledge playful, yet still innocent times. Jack noticed for one brief moment the monster shadow and then it disappeared into the darkness while his companions egged him to put down his blindfold again. His wolf grin was undeniable as he stole another peek to see where Ella had swum to.

"This hungry wolf wants to leave hickeys on all the beautiful girl's necks. Marco." Jack shouted with glee.

"Hey, can't I be nibbled too? Why do the girls get to have all the fun? Polo." Steven shouted.

"Oh don't you worry Steven. I've been eyeballing your thick throat all day. You know I'm going to eat you. Marco." Jack answered very sinisterly back and everyone laughed except Stephen who started moving faster.

"Polo." Everyone shouted but Stephen whispered as he seen Jacks head turn to his direction and move faster. *Yes, that's it Stephen you wanted the wolf; here I come buddy. Wait; something is going on with me. Suddenly, I don't feel so well.* Jack thought as he knew he was going to finally give into Stephen's secret desire and turn him from human into a creature of the night. He was going to bite him for real and drain some of his blood. *Oh no. I need his blood.* Jack ripped off his blindfold.

Just at this moment Jack turned to Mike; and Mike stopped sweet talking Selena and ran out of the water to the empty bottle of magic toad tea. Mike held up the bottle while Jack said the magic word *"reveal"*; and they both saw the poisonous worm chomped in half at the bottom. Then the anger started gaining momentum in Jack's red eyes and Mike looked mortified. Jack suddenly let out a painful scream that became a loud sinister howl. He bent over and started transforming to a more demon looking werewolf with horns. Everyone screamed as his fangs and claws grew longer. This was the side Jack never showed because the demon in his DNA bloodline was powerful and very blood-lustful. He howled again and everyone screamed as the pitch hurt their ears. When he stood up his eyes were now flames as he kept his eyes fixed on Stephen and his mouth foamed with the snarl on his lips.

"Everyone run. This isn't a drill. Someone tried to poison us all and succeeded with Jack. Run and hide or else we are all meat for the beast." Mike yelled and grabbed Selena's hand in a run.

Then Jack let out such a ghastly howl that everyone started running and hiding for real. The game had just taken a turn for the worse as they heard Jack's growl and his rumbling stomach.

Quite unexpectedly as everyone ran from Jack, one person was running towards the monster that continued to foam at the mouth in hunger. Jack filled with pure hatred and hunger; watched as Azriella took off her large silver hoop earrings and magically crafted them to one long silver rope. Jack tried to swipe at her with his long black claws. When he missed she took her chance and bound his arms tight; making him fall hard on his stomach to the earth. The magic of the silver reacted to his black fur transforming him back to human and started burning his skin as beads of sweat rolled off his back.

"I have seen this before. Don't worry the poison is being burned away by the silver and his fast healing. He will be able to enjoy the night with us in about an hour." Ella shouted as she sat on Jack keeping him to the ground as he moaned in human form.

Jack felt a towel covering him and then he felt Mike sitting on his back with Ella, while he looked to the side in agony. The white smoke from his flesh burning didn't erase the hunger as he tried to snap anyone that got to close to his human mouth with elongated fangs. He couldn't switch off his anger. It was like Jack could view what was going on but had no control over what was happening to him. But Mike and Ella tossed him marshmallows that he chomped on viciously.

"Okay, don't worry folks. Jack is under control thanks to Ella. Now, let's torture Jack with some campfire songs. Where did that guitar go?" Mike shouted as Jack groaned.

"Please anything but that." Jack growled.

"But Buddy, I love you and I have to be here for you. Don't worry I grabbed my Dad's mickey of toad tea so you can be happy again later. Now let me sing to you some favorite love songs of mine. Let me begin with my personal favorite folksong; *Grandma got eaten by a Werewolf one Christmas Eve.*" Mike said very grizzly and everyone started laughing except Jack who was trying to chomp unsuccessfully at Mike's werewolf ankles.

🌾🌾🌾🌾

CHAPTER 25

OLLIE

The night air was incredibly hot and it was only the middle of June. But Ollie was completely cheerful as he started digging the grave and every now and then he would watch his friend munch on Ms. Merriweather. *I can't even remember the last time I felt this happy. Everything just feels so surreal; so absolutely wonderful.*

Ollie stopped singing to himself and shoveling dirt as he suddenly felt a cool breeze on his face. He looked up to see Midnight hovering gently across from him. They were just standing there in one moment looking at each other as Ollie smiled over to his wondrous friend and Midnight smiled and nodded back. No words were spoken just the soft sounds of large wings gently beating so quietly they barely could be heard. The breeze surrounded Ollie like a cool embrace from Midnight's ghost of a shadow. And Ollie closed his eyes as he surrendered to this feeling of love in the current of air surrounding him in the lantern lit graveyard.

"Ollie she tasted like chicken but had so many hints and flavors rolled into one. At one point she even tasted a bit like that of a powdered donut. So you might have been right about raising my cholesterol. But it was all for the greater good. In eating Ms. Merriweather I am saving myself from eating countless other lost souls in this wicked town." Midnight said as he grinned.

"I don't think I'd like the taste of Ms. Merriweather. I hated that woman. She was so mean and I hated the fact she didn't give you that recipe you asked so nicely for. But I have a surprise for you. I confiscated something for you." Ollie said as he removed a piece of paper from his pocket and held it out for Midnight.

Midnight looked very mischievous as he floated gently still above the ground and took the piece of paper that looked like it was ancient. Then Ollie watched his friend unfold the paper very carefully and look at what was written. There seemed to be a quiet excitement rising from the dark creature Ollie noticed; as his friend's wings and large bat like ears looked like they had perked up.

"How did you attain such magic?" Midnight was shocked.

"With news of her passing, someone left her back door unlocked so I helped myself to that and some cookies. If you see the Sheriff don't let him know okay?" Ollie said with a grin and put his head down to begin shoveling but took a quick glance over to his demon friend.

"You know most days my human; I dream about draining your blood and offering you mine to gift you immortality. From this day forward all you have to do is think the word 'eternity' and I will understand and gift you eternal life." Midnight sounded so dark but held this warm light in his eyes.

Ollie shrugged his shoulders and turned away chocking back his feelings.

"Immortality is overrated, I think. Only the cool kids get to die young. Besides with the life I had previously lived, I couldn't endure that kind of forever loneliness." Ollie said as he still kept his head down and made real progress on the first grave.

Ollie glanced quickly up to see his great friend still smiling at him. And he watched Midnight carefully fold the paper back and tuck it in his satchel. But the smile never left Ollie's face or Midnights. It was that same smile that frightened him on many occasions but had won his heart many times over as well. *Thank you; thank you, thank you Midnight. I know you can hear me as I speak through my thoughts to you; please know the words I can't speak out loud. Thank you for saving me my friend. I love you Dad.* Ollie kept his head down as he started digging harder and coughed harshly while wiping some tears away.

Ollie couldn't look up as he felt the demon's knarly clawed hand patting his shoulder and give it a squeeze.

Then the breeze Midnight was orchestrating dispersed and Ollie could hear the crickets come back to life in the graveyard. That was when he looked up and seen that his father figure friend had flew away. It was better this way because Ollie still had to finish the first grave and still dig another. *Midnight was right the ground is soft but the dirt is like cement. Time is passing but this is the work of Gods. I love my life finally. I have a future.* As Ollie was in retrospection he looked over to Ms. Merriweather's re-buried grave. *Here I thought Midnight was just trying to give me some night time air with his wings and now I see he was helping me re-bury Ms. Merriweather.*

🌾🌾🌾🌾

Hours went by as Ollie worked diligently finally finishing up and he only patted down the dirt on Ms. Merriweather's grave. He then pulled out the fine silk handkerchief that held the initials *A. P.* and a crown embroidered on it. Leaning on the shovel he dabbed the back of his sweat drenched neck and then looked closer at the stone before him.

The old marble tombstone had a sweet little bird etched into it. The wings were spread open and it looked as if the bird was soaring free through a gray swirling sky. The details were so fine and delicate. He couldn't help but touch the engraved feathers and smile at its beauty.

When he stood up he really took in his surroundings, looking across the new section and the church way up on the hill far away. He heard a long wolf howling in the distance and it made him smile. The moon wasn't full but the darkness was lit up. The fields seemed to blink alive every now and then across the fresh cut grass and up into the night sky. The twinkling was magnetic as he started his journey walking towards his new home and the fireflies were blinking to him on his way. He felt full of purpose and completely at peace in this new world of which he had forgotten for a time. He knew he was completely happy as he smiled at the bright lights. *It's funny how I hadn't realized before how beautiful the world could be at this hour.* Ollie thought as he hummed while making his way to his cabin.

Ollie was so joyous he didn't have a care in the world as he had a bounce in his step walking closer and closer to the cabin. *Oh, shoot I forgot to tell Midnight I can come over next weekend for Father's day. I can't wait to give him the outhouse calendar I bought him. He's going to love it. Okay before I go to the station; I am going to get undressed and have a quick shower. Then I'm going to put on my new shirt and jeans that Midnight bought me as an early birthday present. Oh what a wonderful night. The world really is a good place. I love my life and I am never going to take it for granted again. From this day on I am a new man. Dreams can come true.* Ollie thought as he leaned the shovel up against the door of his little cottage.

Ollie stepped inside and closed the door firmly as he quickly started to undress before he had even flickered on the light. He hummed to himself as he stripped down to his shirt and boxers; and then flipped the switch. As the light turned on Ollie turned around in discarding his shirt and met the shadowy figure that had been moving towards him silently in the dark.

Just as Ollie looked up in horror he gasped at the green monster's cruel face and rippling abs. Just before he could cry for help; the figure hit him hard on the head and then there was only darkness.

🌿🌿🌿

CHAPTER 26

THE WITCHES

"My Love you really screwed up. First off you aren't even supposed to be here. What are you doing? Did I not make the plan clear enough for you? You were supposed to go to the caves in the mountains; by coming here you have put us all in grave danger. Secondly, you have grabbed the wrong guy. How hard is it to distinguish between an eighteen year old werewolf and a twenty-three year old human? Did you not notice when you were beating this human to a pulp that he was fragile? Look at him he is near death. This wasn't part of the plan." Lucinda yelled and was so furious she threw her tea cup out the window.

"Isn't this the right Son? He had the handkerchief with Pendragon's initials. This would only be a gift of love from the King."

"Yes Dufferin, it is from the King to this human. But this isn't the only handkerchief that was given. You have taken the wrong Son. This is his adopted Son. He has only just been accepted by the King these last ten years. What have you done? It looks and sounds like you have broken a rib into his lungs you fool." Lucinda shouted as Dufferin looked distraught at the human that was beaten up and on the table top.

Lucinda gasped as she placed her glowing hand over the body that was struggling to breathe.

"He is suffering. You weren't supposed to kill him. You were supposed to keep him hidden in the mountains for a few days and knock him unconscious if he tried to escape." Lucinda yelled as she pulled her hair out.

"It was an accident. I did hit him unconscious and then he escaped from me and tripped on the jagged rocks along the foot path of the mountain and started gasping. I hit him to try to make him stop making so much noise. This isn't what I wanted Lucinda. My appearance scared the mortal and now he surely will die unless we do something. I couldn't take him to the cave to hide him. He needs too much medical help. He needs magic." Dufferin started shouting back as he was panicked looking at the human struggling to breathe.

There was this unholy gurgling coming from the body on the table top as the human coughed up blood.

"We have to figure out what to do fast. I felt the dark force enter into town and it is moving. It knows we are trying to start the war and destroy its plan. It is coming for us." Hexia said as she watched her sister and her new bumbling buffoon of a brother-in-law standing over the almost dead human on the table.

Hexia turned back to the window in disgust of what was happening and knowing their demise was coming. She seemed to be in a trance as she watched the shaped clouds slowly passing in the dark sky of the early morning and one of the clouds reminded her of her deceased pet crow.

"Dufferin you know I love you but you should also have known that he was human when he didn't heal in your presence. Didn't you realize a human couldn't possible win a fight with a warrior ogre? Even with his cracked ribs; you have broken his arm in three different places and fractured his ankle. His face is all bruised, bloodied, and swelled; he never had a chance. And where are all his clothes? He is in his boxers. The only thing I know is that human teens dress is layers. This is a man or what is left of him and he is definitely human. I can smell his death upon him." Lucinda said solemnly as she listened to the gurgling sounds.

Dufferin deeply frowned as he sank down in a mushroom-stool chair. Suddenly the Old Crone came back from her pizza and tea delivery. She gasped at seeing the almost dead human on her tabletop.

"What has happened? I delivered the tea potion and the boy should have been easy pickings for you. This isn't the last King's Son." The Old Crone's raspy voice was hysterical.

"Sister we are deciding what to do. Should we heal this human with a potion? He will perish within hours if not cared for and even then it is foretold. If we change his fate now the entire world will be sacrificed." Lucinda said as she placed Dufferin's head against her heart in comforting him.

Dufferin although distraught quite enjoyed having his face so close to his wife's large bosom and completely forgot the situation and peril they were in for the moment as he closed his eyes. Instead he was trying to forget the part he played in this catastrophe of all screw ups.

Hexia walked over and put a cold cloth on the human's forehead as the being still struggled to breathe.

"I think we should bury the body and let the creatures of the woods have him. We are doomed either way. But some deaths are more gruesome than others. If the dark force catches us now we shall be tortured in the cruelest of fashions sisters, before he slits our throats and drinks of our life force. And if the supreme council of witches catches us we will be beheaded. Either way our death approaches. But I can tell you if the Demon King shall find us first before all others; we will wish and pray we were never born. He has the powers to raise the dead and torture us for all of eternity in the deepest pits of Hell for killing his Son. For even though this human named Oliver River is adopted; he is the King of Avalon's Son; this is just as true as the blood in my veins. I know this my sisters." Hexia said in a hush as even the Devil himself was listening.

Hexia went back to the window as she looked out to the shadows of the forest that used to give her comfort and now seemed terrifying as they danced in the windows light.

Dufferin had been listening and watching when all the witches started pacing back and forth. He was guilty and hoped for a solution. The only thing he knew was that he was completely in love with Lucinda. When he looked up though instead of Lucinda's sweet face greeting him in comfort again; it was the Old Crone who had stopped before him in a sneer.

"Dufferin you should never have brought him here." The Old Crone was cruel in her tone and stuck her razor sharp nail and bony finger into the flesh of Dufferin's nose making it bleed little drops of green blood.

"There is no need to curse the damned sister. Come Dufferin and let us think of a solution." Lucinda said in a hiss as she removed her sister's nail from out of Dufferin' skin.

Then Lucinda proceeded to kiss him feverishly like no one was in the room and Dufferin kissed her back just as passionately. The lovers were holding and kissing each other completely ignoring the situation and everyone. The Old Crone and Hexia rolled their eyes at the two sneaking away to the bedroom and the loud sounds of furniture breaking.

Hexia and the Old Crone turned their backs on the closed door and worked a sleeping spell over the almost dead body so they could buy a little more time in figuring out what to do.

"I've got it. We should let him die and then use the necromancer potion. Then we could have him as a zombie servant. I give him days and even less than that if we bury him alive." Hexia said with excitement completely ignoring the truth in their situation and jumped up and down clapping her hands.

"What are you dense sister? We shall not even be around in days. No potions can fix our death in the prophesy. Besides, that spelled potion has too much pizazz for this human. Do you want him to become a pole dancing zombie-stripper?" The Old Crone cackled but Hexia didn't laugh and the others were going for round two by the sounds of pottery shattering.

"That is true sister. I had forgotten the flash mob of 1978. It was disco music till dawn." Hexia said completely looking miserable as she glared at the floor.

"Forget that. I'd rather be burned alive by the townsfolk." The Old Crone said in grief.

🌾🌾🌾🌾

Dufferin and Lucinda walked into the kitchen with rosy cheeks and big smiles. Completely in love and temporarily disregarding the grave situation they were all in. And Hexia and the Old Crone looked at them both in disgust as they continued talking only to each other.

Just now; the discussion had turned to how the Devil invented disco music to torture mortals and it had the reverse effect on evolved creatures. Dufferin smiled even more because in the deepest part of his soul he cherished anything disco; including balls and bell bottom pants.

"Please…please…kill me. The pain is too great for an *eternity* without him." Ollie coughed up more blood as it spurted from his mouth and broke the sleeping spell.

It was his soul that was crying for mercy and everyone gasped. Time was almost up.

🌾🌾🌾🌾

CHAPTER 27

MIDNIGHT

The coffee and blood was going down slow this morning as I re-read the piece of parchment containing the doomsday puzzle. I couldn't stop thinking about Ollie. Leaving the human was hard; it had been hard since the moment I found him. He was such a free spirit and very stubborn. Ollie had felt like he was betraying his deceased parents and used to fight me on everything; even when being frightened of me. Even in his loneliness; I had only convinced him to move in with us for the first seven years out of the ten I've known him for. But he was so determined to make something out of his life and I had to respect his wishes.

And now he had done it; he was sober. He was twenty-three and the man I had always hoped he'd become. And he had finally accepted me as the father I was to him. But I felt like my human was leaving me as I flew. He was leaving me behind in his quest for happiness.

It was getting even harder leaving him to be human and fragile. But it was because he finally realized what I was to him and what he was to me. I was so proud of him for not giving up even though I almost lost him a few times.

Yesterday morning and this morning, I could feel Ollie's abundant glee radiating out of him as if his soul was the sun. I just wanted to linger in that light of purity a little while longer.

But something evil has been in town and it has been hidden. It was the great evil force that the prophesy spoke of. The prophesy has to be fulfilled; it cannot be changed or denied any further. Over three hundred years has passed since I travelled from across the ocean to get to the place where the gateway would open. I have looked over this damn scroll for centuries and yet still I am no further to solving its secret, its riddle. I wish Merlin was still here; for his guidance was always cherished.

All this time I thought the oracle was speaking about Julia and our unwavering love for each other. All I see is the sun setting and rising in her adoring eyes. But this isn't talking about her. This is about someone else close to me.

Normally I looked quite ordinary in my human form except my fangs which could not be hidden and as I was frustrated they grew longer. I could feel my fangs getting jagged as I gritted them. My uniform had been pressed and the pentagram on my chest seemed to have a glow around it from the power I gave it. But I sighed loudly in the empty office. I sat at the desk studying the ancient burnt scroll and read aloud the only words visibly legible in hopes that this time I would find the missing piece to a giant puzzle of how the world would end. But more than anything I looked for a great clue at how I could save the world. Even though I had read the scroll a million times before and re-read the scroll aloud a trillion times. Time was up and I knew it; so I read it out loud again.

"The rising sun will set on a delicate love so fair,

The darkness creeps in with unbalanced fury care,

The end of the world begins on the back of a pregnant unicorn mare,

The dead shall rise and hell's army gates will open rare,

All is doomed unless the King's heart of armor answers the prayer." My voice was deep and clear and it echoed ominously off the station walls.

Then I slammed my fist hard on the table leaving the wood cracked in half where my skin had connected. I thought back to the witch that wanted to mate with me before she gave me the scroll. It was a different time back then and we were both burning in hell but I refused her and she cursed me as I was sent back to earth to be an abomination in this dimension. *Why the hell do these prophesies have to be riddled lines of garbage made from horny celibate witches who dream of having their way with vampires and the world pays when they can't? The only thing this is missing is the blood sacrifice of the world on a silver platter. I guess I was fortunate to steal it away with me when the other witches raised me from the grave. But this great apocalypse has been coming on for centuries. Centuries and centuries of battling Generals sent from hell to force me into the war and kill off humanity. Was it all because she couldn't get laid?* My thoughts were ranting to myself in frustration and I changed focus to start cracking eggs for my colleague that should be joining me soon.

I had the bacon frying already and everything was going to be ready in perfect timing. I made the plate fancy and buttered the toast putting a little bit of strawberry jam on the bread; just the right amount that Ollie liked. When the breakfast was finished and on the plate; it looked like a masterpiece. The bacon made the smile complete and the eggs were the perfect golden eyes. The toast halves were ears. It looked very comical but I deeply enjoyed making this meal for Ollie because I knew how much my human enjoyed it.

I poured the orange juice and then sat back down making myself another half mixture of blood and coffee. I needed the extra kick as the night was almost over. I looked back over the ancient scroll turning the burnt edges carefully to see if there was something I missed all these years.

But nothing came to my mind except the strange looking blood splatter across the writing. The more I looked at the blood that seemed to fade into purple blobs; the more it resembled the shape of a giant dragon. Only I knew the traitor's blood of whom I had withdrew Excalibur and wounded the fiend indefinitely. I damned that individual in a prison in the deepest part of hell where he would be ripped over and over or worse; he would be subjected to sleep with that demented demon witch. It was always the worse of the two; although sometimes hell liked to play both in being theatrically humorous.

I glanced at the clock on the wall and stood up so fast my chair hadn't noticed and was knocked to the ground. The clock started chiming four times. And throughout my mind I heard Ollie's voice say the word; *"eternity."*

≹≹≹≹

CHAPTER 28

THE WITCHES

The ogre warrior was a shell of his worth and seemed to crumble at hearing the human's faint plea. Dufferin covered his face and started to cry. Lucinda went over to him and started rubbing his back in comforting him. She then held him so tight but it was to no avail. Dufferin was beside himself.

"There, there precious it's not your fault." Lucinda said as she tried to hold him tighter but Dufferin broken free from her comfort.

"All of you don't understand. I can feel this human's heart giving out and when he perishes it is on my soul. With the dark stain this will leave on my heart; I will never be allowed back into my kingdom. I will never see my homeland again. I will be an outcast in breaking the ogre code of cease-fire; the code I have sworn my whole life to. Bloodshed has never been my tribe's motto; peaceful resolutions have always been what we are committed to seek and I have broken my life values."

Dufferin cried out.

"All of us are outcasts including this human. He only has a few moments left and if we save his life by magic he will forever be changed. A seed of darkness will spread in his good heart. The seed will be sprung from our meddling and trying to save our punishments; instead of saving his life because it is the right thing to do. There is only one way now and that is to let him die. We won't kill him or help save him; anymore interference from us will only make his death or life worse." Hexia spoke as she turned to the look out into the darkness of the forest.

"Kidnapping was bad enough; but death and interference with the mortal realm has tarnished all our souls. Dufferin all our fates were tied the moment you brought him through our door and laid him out on our wooden table." The Old Crone spoke through gritted teeth as she gave them all angry glances.

Then she stormed out of the cabin slamming the door hard as she left. The disgust of this buffoonery had caused a vile taste in her mouth and she puked just outside. She wiped her mouth on her long black sleeve and then went to the magic well in the middle of the yard to bring up the bucket.

The bucket wasn't full of water instead it held a steel magic sword that shone like the onyx eyes of a black widow. The black of the steel was tarnished and oozed of evil sludge. The sword was made from the very first witch in the fires of hell. The demon witch was the twin sister of the Lady of the Lake and her name was the Fury of the Flames. The metal had been stolen from a great sin; still containing the blood of Christ. The special sword was re-forged in hell and named; the Luciforge or the Spear of Destiny. This was the equal sword in power to Excalibur and was the only weapon to use against the King Demon of Avalon and all the vampires. At the very destruction of the world the witches were planning on slaying the King.

Plans had changed though. The Old Crone took the sword with her and got into her car. *There is only one thing to do. I have to go where the teenagers are playing games. I have to kill the son Dufferin was supposed to take in the first place. I am already damned; this is just going to ensure the rage of the Last King in order to defeat the evil villain now here in town.* The Old Crone thought these thoughts as she sped off to the quarry filled with unsuspecting teenagers. She smoked her old pipe so much that a cloud hovered around her head as she raced through the woods.

She made it to the clearing and then went in on foot to not provoke the werewolves that were partying. She had the advantage as she was downwind of the teens and hid behind a huge red oak. She noticed the faint protection spell placed over the quarry but was able to easily break a hole in the rising purple fog with her sword.

She was watching the teens playing around in the water. *Up all hours of the night. Youth really is wasted on the young.* The Old Crone thought as she saw her target that was now being chased by a fairy that aggressively tackled him to the shore and attacked him with kisses. *What an unholy abomination of love. I shall smite thee young Prince of Darkness for thy greater good of the world.* The Old Crone thought as she raised the sword and was going to charge but some unseen force stopped her in her tracks.

🌾🌾🌾🌾

CHAPTER 29

LANCELOT

The Old Crone stood there frozen and she gasped but nothing came out of her mouth. Her sword was thrown to the ground and her black cloak was taken from her leaving her stripped and magically suspended in the air.

"Merrideath, why are you concealed from me in this old skin as a disguise? This is not your true-form. I shall reveal myself now entirely so you should know your captor and your death." He was deeply angry and his voice was cold and hard; as he stood before her wearing a straw hat.

Suddenly he sliced her stomach with her own sword and all her old skin fell away to reveal a beautiful woman who looked no more than thirty but was actually centuries old. He discarded his disguise of the old Farmer Magland's skin he was in. He stepped into the light for her to see his armor that held an inverted black cross and his evil fanged grin towards her. He threw the sword down as his red eyes glared at her.

"Lancelot." She gasped before he grabbed her by the throat and held her high in front of him.

"Merrideath you disgust me. Look at what you have become. You were trying to ruin me but I knew you would come to kill the Son. I was summoned as soon as you broke my fake protection spell. You were trying to stop me. But you are too weak. The only thing you are good for is my breakfast. You shall die knowing that I am going for your sisters next and they will taste better than you ever did. Remember that night we shared so long ago? It was only to gain the secrets of the Luci-forge sword that you have brought to me now. I was never in love with you. I was with Hexia this whole time. She is the only one that I have ever loved and we are secretly wed. She gave up your great plan easily over some afternoon delight. Let your last breath know how much I hate you and how much I am going to make the others pay for crossing me." Lancelot angrily whispered in her ear as a magic mirror suddenly appeared where he could see his reflection and hers.

He then sank his fangs into her neck hard and started to drain her as her wide eyes looked on. Suddenly with the last piece of her strength she closed her eyes and summoned her sword to her hand as she forced it into his groin.

"I shall die but you shall never make love to another. And hear me now Lancelot. You will be stopped. The light always conquers the darkness; and that was what the prophesy foretold on the scroll. That is why it was burned in the fires of hell and even then it couldn't be fully destroyed. There are many prophesies but in all of them you die; limp and unloved." Merrideath cackled and was immediately released as Lancelot fell to his knees.

His ears started to bleed in hearing her truth and she continued to cackle dying on the forest floor as he focused on stopping the bleeding from his groin. His anguish turned to hatred again as rushed to her and tore out her laughing throat. Then he ripped open her chest and ate her heart. This action set her body on fire as she immediately turned to ashes.

"You don't know anything Merrideath. In fact you have given me the one weapon I needed to stop Excalibur and slay the King." Lancelot whispered out of anger and wiped the blood tears from his eyes.

He spit on her ashes that started blowing away in the wind. Then he focused on the teenagers and Pendragon's Son. Instead of rushing in to kill them all; he raised his bloodied hand and said a magic spell to keep the teenagers safe as long as they stayed in the quarry. All of the evil creatures would be unleashed today but not here. He had other plans for Jack which involved raising him to be a General for hell. He knew he could easily persuade the other teens and use them for his new army.

He quickly left in his shadow form using a healing spell to seal up his giant wound. He stopped and felt Jack's gaze on him but he was faster in disappearing from the teen's view. Even walking with a limp in his step couldn't stop his thirst for vengeance; and his rush to Merrideath's junk of a car. The car was parked further away than he would like it to be but still he couldn't contain his momentum.

🌾🌾🌾

All he had to do now was hope that the human named Ollie was still alive so he could turn him immortal. When Lancelot got out of the car he could see his beautiful bride with her long raven hair standing by the window in the cabin. The cabin was hidden far into the woods but he had always known where it was. *It's too bad she doesn't fit into my plan. There are only two beings which I need right now and then my plan will be complete. They can't be away from each other; this treachery of putrid love is perfect. I wish I had more time; Lucinda is ripe. She is way too powerful to be with that giant dope. There might be time to make her my love-slave. Maybe that would be a nice change to my plans. Either way this morning is going to be glorious.* Lancelot thought as he transformed into Merrideath and set off some fireworks.

The others came out of the cabin looking at Merrideath astonished.

"What are you doing sister? And why are you not in your Old Crone disguise anymore?" Lucinda said and immediately stopped the fireworks and then turned to see her husband ogling her sister.

"I am tired of hiding my beauty. If our death is near than I want to show my true-form. I have an idea. I think we should go to where the real Son is and ambush him as leverage for our lives. We should forget the human to his fate. He is lost but the other Son is not." Merrideath said with her youthful alluring voice that made Dufferin lose his breath and take a second glance at her while she winked.

"I think that might work out but we must prepare. Merrideath take Dufferin up to the mountain where our weapons are hidden. Lucinda and I will gather ingredients and make some potions to plan our attack on the evil presence in town." Hexia said as she quickly took Lucinda's hand and went back to the garden to get the herbs and weeds for the potion.

"Okay my love I will be back soon." Dufferin said as he followed his sister in-law deeper into the thick woods and up the mountain to a small cave entrance secretly hidden by giant orange mushrooms.

As Merrideath said the magic words the ancient stone door opened and then closed as soon as they stepped inside.

"Oh no, the door closed. Can the door be unlocked from our side Merrideath?" Dufferin was frightened as he tried to pull the unmoving stone.

"Yes silly. It can only be moved by magic." Merrideath's voice changed to a raspy sultry tone and Dufferin was frightened as his mind wandered to unknown thoughts in the darkness.

"I need the light. I can't see. Where are you Merrideath?" Dufferin said in panic as he reached out and touched the softest skin he had ever touched in his life.

"Where has your cloak gone Merrideath? Your skin is softer than all the fabrics in my kingdom. I am sorry. I know I shouldn't." Dufferin stammered as he felt her hands on his chest and abs.

Her curves were firm and he couldn't stop from squeezing and grabbing the mounds of pleasure. He felt equally soft hands caressing his body and taking off his loin cloth and armor. He heard the ache in his throat as even though he wished to stop he couldn't and his lips found hers in the darkness.

"We are dead anyways Dufferin. Let me have you to hold in my loneliness as a secret treasure to my grave. I need you now to take me. Take all your forbidden passion out on my flesh. I have seen the way you have looked at me when I bathed in the river all those times and I have felt all of your stolen touches to my skin in ecstasy. Grant me my dying wish." Merrideath sweetly said as Dufferin gave into her without any reservation at all.

His moan was loaded as he frantically kept going; unable to stop even though he needed to catch his breath. He was under some kind of fever and his heart felt betrayed because he couldn't get enough of Merrideath. As she slammed him to the ground she started kissing his lower body with her satin lips and he couldn't stop gasping for air. Suddenly the torches were full and the fire smoldered the space as he looked at a giant magic mirror which showed the two of them on the stone floor.

Dufferin gasped as his neck was bleeding and he looked ghostly white. Then he looked at Merrideath and she seemed to have red glowing eyes as she moved her sweet lips feverishly. She was making him about to explode and then he felt sharp agony instead of a sweet release. He looked at their image in the mirror in horror and followed the trail of blood flowing down from between his legs. It was the most excruciating pain that he had ever felt in his life as he tried to scream but nothing came. Then a moment later his throat was torn out.

Lancelot transformed and started laughing at the ogre's wide eyes in the mirror seeing his bloody dismembered prized jewel just before he died. *Wow, ogres really are tasty. I will have to make a mental note to capture as many as I can and keep them separately as my toys.* Lancelot thought as he grinned. *One down, two more to go.* Lancelot quickly transformed to Dufferin and put on his loin cloth and armor. *There's nothing much to these garments. What is the point of partial armor if you have no protection for the most important thing on your body?* Lancelot thought in frustration as he grabbed the Luci-forge sword and strapped it to his back. But before he did; he stopped in the mirror and lifted the flap of his loin cloth to really get a look at himself. He had to make sure everything was intact and working as he gave himself a good couple of strokes. *That bitch couldn't hurt me. There's only a small scar. I'm okay. I'm fine. Okay, now to kill another bitch of a sister off.* Lancelot said as he punched himself in the groin to control his excitement and kill his enthusiasm.

It worked as he slowly made his way out of the cave. He magically closed the entrance and gave himself a couple of aspirins to stop the pain he just inflicted. *Okay next time I don't have to punch that hard. But I am so exultant things are working out amazingly. It's like all of hell is smiling at me now and cheering me on.* Lancelot thought as he walked as Dufferin but with a limp and tried to hide his huge grin.

❦❦❦

He cleared his throat and straightened his uniform pausing outside the small cabin. He thought of his possible death and that wiped his smile off his face for now. Although it was just temporary because he knew he was going to win this war. *I can't be stopped now. I am just too wonderful. I simply am the most magnificent creature of creatures. I can't wait. Okay, I have to focus. I have to be a stupid ogre like Dufferin now.* Lancelot thought as he straightened himself again. He frowned as he walked inside the front door to the cabin.

"Ladies, I have brought the weapon. I think we might need some provisions for our journey." Dufferin said as his frown looked painful.

"Where is Merrideath?" Hexia said as she looked out the window.

"Oh, she needed you to find her the wintergreen. She said in the darkness of the morning her eyesight is poor and she can't seem to find it on the forest floor." Dufferin said with a sigh.

"Why didn't you show her where it is? We have all walked these woods millions of times." Hexia said and rolled her eyes.

"Hexia just go with Dufferin to get Merrideath so I can finish this potion. We don't have that much time." Lucinda said in frustration as she listened to the human barely hanging on but still fought.

"Fine. I shall go with this big brute. But you know the wintergreen has to be washed in the river before we use it. The well water has been polluted with fairy blood." Hexia said and rolled her eyes again.

"Okay. Just go and comeback quickly." Lucinda said as she sighed while using her mortar and pestle fanatically crushing flowers.

"I shall see you soon my love." Dufferin said as he walked over and kissed Lucinda deeply making Hexia blush.

"I'm leaving now." Hexia said and then Dufferin quickly followed her out the door while hearing a heavenly sigh from Lucinda.

Hexia lead the way along the river bank exactly to where the wintergreen was and plucked a bunch for the potion. Dufferin held out the large basket where she put the plants as they walked along the river.

"Where is Merrideath? I thought you said she would be here." Hexia said and looked around for her sister but there was no one there except Dufferin.

"Oh I forgot to tell you, she said she would catch up with us but needed some kind of sword in the cave." Dufferin said and his voice seemed unexpectedly more inviting to Hexia.

"Oh yes. That sword is her favorite weapon. It was created by our mother. It has a name; it's called the Luci-forge and it was created using the blade from the Spear of Destiny. Merrideath has used it many times to dismember males that cross her." Hexia said and laughed.

She blushed in seeing Dufferin dipping his toes in the river while he gave her the basket.

"That seems very cruel Hexia. How do you feel about the male species?" Dufferin said as he slowly took off his armor and then his loin cloth.

He turned in all his glory to face Hexia who was severely blushing now.

"What are you doing Dufferin? You don't have to be naked to wash the wintergreen. I can be; as you have seen me a million times before in the river. Besides, what if an eel mistakenly takes a bite from you?" Hexia asked in a hush tone as he took the basket from her hands and set it on the forest floor.

Then he undid her black cloak letting it fall to the ground and she didn't stop him. He took her hand and pulled her into the river with him. He started kissing her very delicately and she started kissing him back immediately. He didn't even have to use the same love spell on Hexia she was already melting in his hands.

"I knew it was you lover. I knew you were in disguise. Lucinda doesn't deserve your love like I do. I am way prettier than Lucinda and stronger too. I won't break like she would." Hexia said between slightly moaning to his touches.

The two were rough as they couldn't get enough of each other moving quickly and harder in the water.

"Oh my Hexia; you have seduced my innocence yet again and again." Dufferin said out of breath and then burst with a low moan.

But he placed his hand over her mouth while she cried out in pleasure. Then as she relaxed more in his painful grip he pushed her hard under the water. He held her under the water as she frantically tried to free herself. Then he transformed back to his true-self as her eyes went wide and eventually she stopped fighting him. The one thing he didn't count on was his uncontrollable sobbing as he still held her down but she wasn't moving. Her stare back to him was blank.

He picked her up and blood tears started flowing out of his eyes as he sank his fangs into her neck draining her blood completely.

"My true love you were never part of my plan and I can't afford you to screw up my destiny of ruling this world." Lancelot said as he held Hexia's dead body a little longer.

His tears were real as he covered her back up in her black cloak and moved her body to an unmarked grave he had dug days before. He still ripped out her black heart and ate it. But she did not burst into flames; instead her chest held a hollowed out hole from her missing heart. He gently placed her in the grave and used his claw to drop a few precious splatters of his blood in her open chest. Then he supernaturally filled the grave with layers and layers of dirt. He washed himself off and then transformed back to his Dufferin disguise.

He was going back to the cabin now. *I shall see you soon my love, when I raise the others. Now there is only one sister left and she is the only one that Matters. For the spell to work it has to be the blood of true love's betrayal.* He thought as he grinned in the darkness and practically skipped to the cabin. He adjusted his feelings to hide his happiness just before he got to the steps of the cabin and tried to remember to be weak and stupid like Dufferin was; for the disguise to work.

❦❦❦❦

"Lucinda, I'm back. Our sisters told me to tell you they would meet you in town by the bowling alley. How is the human?" Dufferin said sounding distraught.

"He is almost gone Dufferin. I tried healing him enough to keep him alive a little longer but he is just passing now." Lucinda said and Dufferin started crying and turned from her.

"It's okay my love. Hey there baby; its okay." Lucinda walked over to the great ogre and he placed his arms around her; kissing her in-between tears.

"I'm so scared Lucinda. I don't know what's going to happen to us. And it feels like forever since I had you alone." Dufferin said still sobbing and closed his eyes as Lucinda started really kissing him back.

"My love we might only have tonight." Lucinda said as she took his hand and pulled him back to their bedroom.

They both started kissing and a love making frenzy succeeded a couple of more times until they both collapsed in each other's exhausted arms. Dufferin seemed completely happy as Lucinda laid her head on his strong chest; and she kissed the place where his heart should have been.

"My Husband, I cannot hear your heartbeat tonight but I felt the hot passion of our love. I can see it in your eyes; it burns as bright as red flames. You have never been so aggressive in your loving touches. But tonight has been the best lovemaking of my life. I feel like your spirit is more alive to my body as you have never been before. I am so tired now, we should fall asleep and when death shall come we will not hear its knock at the door." Lucinda said as Dufferin sank his teeth in her neck drinking her blood but all she felt was ecstasy in his kiss not pain. She was completely oblivious to the fact he had just drank a lot of her blood to make her weaker. Her eyes remained closed as she was completely content and felt so deadly tired.

"Third wife of mine; if tonight is our last night let us sacrifice ourselves in the heat of passion and display our love to the world. It will be our last tribute to our marriage instead of dying by the hands of the supreme council or dying by the evil awaiting to catch us." Dufferin said and then suddenly got up and started getting dressed.

He looked over at the luscious curves of Lucinda's sweating, tired body and frowned. Her large doe eyes were so pretty, as was her full lips but he still scowled as he threw her black dress at her.

"We need to go to the mountain. Merrideath gave me the only weapon we need. We need to leave everything behind now." Dufferin said in a more assertive voice and Lucinda did as commanded of her; slipping the dress over her head.

"I can no longer hear the human. He is already passed on now. Our plan will work regardless my love. Couldn't we spend our last few hours here together? Dufferin what do you mean third wife?" Lucinda said as she placed her hand on Dufferin's arm gently trying to pull him back to her.

"No Lucinda. If you love me, you will show me. I do not wish to hide any of my marriages. Come with me and let us make love before the mountain. Show me how much you love me or else I am leaving. I do not wish to be your dark secret when I have two others who are willing to please me." Dufferin said as he started walking out the door with the wrapped weapon strapped to his muscular back as Lucinda sat there for a moment shocked at her husband.

She rushed after him leaving the door to the cabin wide open. She was practically running to catch up to him as she tried to grab his hand and he pulled it away from her harshly.

"Of course I love you. But this is a very dark spot in the forest we are entering and witches are supposed to be neutral. It is forbidden for us to be here. I am not ashamed of our love but it will be the end of the world in a couple of hours. Why do we need to prove anything now?" Lucinda said as she ran up ahead of Dufferin's long strides and tried to put her hands out to stop him from going further.

Dufferin stopped only for a moment and slapped her hard across the face.

"Do you not know me at all? I am a Prince among my people and I can have any woman I desire. I have had many women more beauteous than you. Do you think I am going to stay with you, if you can't even prove how much you love me? You told me tonight was the best you have ever had; well I have had better. You are becoming lazy in pleasing me and I will be bored with you if you cannot make love to me tonight on the altar." Dufferin shouted as she was still on the ground.

Her hands were to her face and tears were streaming down.

"But I love you. Don't you know this? Dufferin please don't leave. Our world is ending and I want to be with you." Lucinda pleaded with him as she remained on the forest floor.

Dufferin rolled his eyes in disgust at her pitifulness and started running away from her up to the path that led into the secret grove; where the altar sat above a hill that faced a flat section of the mountain. He could hear Lucinda's frantic footsteps running to catch up with him and he smiled wickedly as his plan was working.

He started to unravel the cloth the sword was in and placed the blade beside the altar; and then he quickly said an ancient spell while the altar glowed with a purple mist. A red outline of a door appeared in the odd flat piece of rock on the mountainside; in front of the stone table. Dufferin didn't wait for her to make up her mind as he started undressing and then reached down to where Lucinda was and lifted her to the rock ledge around the stone table. He lifted her dress over her head and tore it up before throwing it to the ground as she anxiously looked around. She was trying to cover her bountiful curves as she nervously looked around seeing eyes in the woods.

"I can't do this Dufferin. In the old days this was the spot where witches were sacrificed to the Devil. We don't know whose eyes are upon us now. This is a place of pure evil. We must go." Lucinda whispered as she thought she seen a couple of ghosts float by and shivered.

"Kiss me and forget everything. You are already nude and I have just destroyed your dress. We have no other options. Either you make love to me or I am leaving you. I know I am that good looking. I can have anyone I want." Dufferin said as he kissed her and she started kissing him back but shivered with each kiss.

He picked her up again and she kissed him lovingly but he was rough as she opened for him. Even in her tenderness; he placed her hard on the altar and sliced her back off the altar rock. She cried out loud but he didn't stop kissing her as some of her blood trickled across the stone. He was kissed her even harder and she had hesitated at first from the pain but then kissed him back stronger to match his kisses. As he was rough with her; she became weaker but didn't slow down. She wanted him to love her the way he had before. But she slowly realized that he wasn't the knight in shining armor she had married. He wasn't making love to her; this felt like the desperate actions of someone who didn't care.

"Don't make me leave you Lucinda. I am very good. I can find another play toy; you are actually my sixth wife. But you have to trust me. I love you. Besides you don't want to seem weak do you? Hexia told me she was stronger than you and she proved it to me in the river. She screamed my name louder than you ever have. Even Merrideath screamed my name louder than you and she was much softer. Her skin was so lavishing I couldn't keep my hands off her. Making love to her fulfilled my fantasy of making love to the most beautiful witch in the world." Dufferin said as Lucinda started crying and then he made her scream.

He knew he had succeeded. Lucinda was now crying tears of pain at hearing his words. He had successfully betrayed and broke her heart. Just then he transformed into his true-form while taking her harder. Lancelot could see the look in her sad eyes and almost hear the exact moment he broke her spirit and it made him incredibly satisfied. He grinned and sank his teeth in her neck while she screamed even louder but no one could hear her over the otherworldly chanting around the altar. The ghost of minions and ghouls had been circling them and chanting the song to open the hell gate.

Just at the climax of the song; he reached down and pulled out the Luci-forge. Lucinda was so weak while she just looked wide eyed full of tears at Lancelot and he plunged the sword hard into her abdomen. He heard a crunch and a metallic snap as the sword touched through to the other side to the stone. She was pinned and slowly gasped as her blood flowed down into an angled section and straight to the red outlined door frame.

He lifted his hands and finished the spell as the doorframe opened revealing the underworld of fire and brimstone. The loving betrayed blood was the last touch to opening the gateway to hell and a sea of zombies started coming out. Lancelot stood over her corpse laughing as the zombies brought out his new clothes and a new shiny suit of armor. He marveled at the horde of zombies pouring out of the doorway while Lucinda's lifeless body lay sprawled in a bloodbath.

When Lancelot tried to pull the sword out of Lucinda he needed the help of several demons. As they all pulled together; they fell back as it was released and laughed together. But Lancelot gasped as he noticed the missing chunk taken out of the steel. And he didn't have time to find the metal as the horde of zombies and demons feasted on the sacrifice of Lucinda's body. Lancelot even joined in feasting with the other evil creatures as he was uncontrollably famished for the sacrificed witch's flesh that set them all free. *Best sweetness ever. This war is over; first Trenton then the world. I shall have to remember this recipe so I can enjoy this dessert again in the future.* Lancelot thought as he grinned.

🌿🌿🌿🌿

CHAPTER 30

MIDNIGHT

Something was wrong. Ollie hasn't shown up and now it was just past four in the morning. I heard my human say the word and he needs me. I have to find him and gift him immortality. As I was on my way out the door I got two emergency calls to the station; of someone freaking out because there was what looked like zombies rummaging through their trash can; and a zombie trying to eat their cat. I rolled my eyes at this statement but decided to investigate this prank call because of the urgency in the voice over the phone.

I leaped into the patrol truck and sped off towards Ms. Murdoch's countryside house where apparently her cat was stuck up in a tree because a zombie was trying to eat it. *A zombie seriously? Ms. Murdoch's been into the moonshine again. I don't know how many times I have to confiscate her distillery barrels they keep springing up in the back woods. That toad tea tastes like dirty gym socks in my opinion and it doesn't do anything for me. I shall have to find Oliver after. Thank heavens my blood is already in his veins from the cupcake. I mustn't think like this but I have wanted to change him for a long time now. What am I thinking? I want him to be okay and alive. I hope he is okay.* I thought and continued driving.

As I drove I realized the dawn was much more alive than normal. It was only going on 4:20am and I had received three more calls over the C.B. radio. I was only on my way to the first call when Doris the dispatcher had given me two more addresses to check out.

When I finally arrived to the scene of the crime, I could clearly see the back of an individual with a very dirty red and blue striped sweater and black pants. The individual was clearly trying to swipe at the animal that was continuing to climb higher and higher in the large maple.

I flashed the truck's lights as I seen Ms. Murdoch peeking from behind her curtain. The old lady was waving to me and pointing to over on her lawn and then she hid again behind her curtains. I could feel her eyes still watching from the flimsy curtain. *Yes, I see the cat and person.*

I got out of the truck and rushed forward just as the cat fell from the flimsy branch it was clinging to. In a split second, I caught the cat mid-air before it landed in the suspect's arms. And then I turned to face the individual creating all the fuss. The cat was squirming in my death grip and now I could see why.

After being this close I realized the person was a male with green skin. The male's skin was almost slimed as it was missing in patches and worms and centipedes crawled out of it. One of the male suspect's eyes was out of the socket and dangling against their green cheek that was missing the flesh; revealing the bone structure of teeth and a deteriorated jaw. The suspect growled and tried to reach out but I was too fast and the zombie was too slow. *Wow, I guess the old lady was right. There is a zombie in her front yard trying to eat her cat. But the bigger question is; why?* I thought as I slowly walked back to my truck placing the cat inside as I grabbed my baseball bat.

The zombie was making the usual grunting and wailing sounds. It moved slower than molasses on a winter night and it was very easy for me to send the zombie back to where it came from. I connected the bat to the zombie's skull in a grotesque cracking sound that made me smile more than I would like to admit. The zombie had fallen and not gotten up. *Damn zombie. They really are a nuisance more than anything. You can only stop them through severe traumatic blows to the brain or else they keep rising.* As I looked at the lifeless corpse that had been re-animated I contemplated either experimentation or eating what was left. So I threw the lightweight body into the back of the truck just as Ms. Murdoch came out shaking her cane at me.

"You cat thief. Give me back my Reginald or I shall go to the Mayor." Ms. Murdoch's sweet angry elderly voice was so cute that I smiled automatically.

"It's okay Ms. Murdoch, here you go." I said nonchalantly as I opened the door of my truck and the ungrateful cat ran into Ms. Murdoch's house.

Ms. Murdoch didn't stop to say thank you she just turned and walked back into the house slamming the door hard. *She really thought I would steal her cat? I knew it. She was into the moonshine tonight.* I smiled at that thought as I went to a much bigger disturbance that the dispatch gave me of a zombie army trying to break into a school. *I can feel the surge of evil through the town this morning. I have to go to the graveyard right now.* I thought as I called home before I started my vehicle.

"Julia its happening. Stay safe in the house my love; it is magically protected by Jeeves. Or if you must go out remember to aim for the head. Hell has brought forth a legion of zombies to smite me with. I love you, please keep Jack safe and I will try to come home as soon as I can. I have to stop this attack before it is too late. If Ollie comes to the house, make him stay. We need our family safe. I love you my River Maiden." After I left the message I sped down the road to the graveyard for a quick stop.

I parked the truck right on the church lawn. Then I transformed to my vampiric bat-form and flew to the little bunker when I observed the door left ajar. I was shocked as I could see all the signs of a struggle between my friend and some unknown creature. Then I noticed the same clothes Ollie was wearing earlier piled on the floor along with his boots. I looked at the muddy foot prints and noticed the seventh toe on each massive foot. *An ogre...an ogre took my human.* I thought and then suddenly paused gasping at seeing the blood smeared on the floor and inside door.

I roared fiercely to the skies; my anger transformed me immediately up a notch to full out demon vampire as my fangs and claws grew longer; already needing to feed off the vengeance of blood from my enemies. My large wings were up and ready to take flight as I smelt the air of the enemy I was tracking. I hovered outside Ollie's house and deeply inhaled the scent of the enemy and Ollie's blood. I was going to destroy anyone that hurt my human. Just as I was going to take off up the trail of blood and mud into the woods; the priest came out with the largest cross aimed at me.

"Stay back demon, go back to hell." The priest yelled as he came running down the church steps while I stopped, as the priest continued to run and then trip on his long robe.

Just before the priest would have hit the ground I lifted him by his collar. The priest had managed to still raise the cross in my face but I didn't say a word. I just placed my gangly long nail on the cross and it set on fire. As soon as the wood lit up the priest dropped the cross with a scream.

"I have been waiting a long time to eat you my plump friend. But unfortunately, I have pressing Matters of the end of the world to attend to just now. But you can bet your sweet dark-souled-ass that I will be back for you. And if I find out you hurt Oliver in anyway, you will suffer slowly; in unimaginable ways before I devour your heart." I said in my most menacing voice and the priest was visibly shaking as I let him go and he dropped to the ground.

"I am not afraid of the place I shall go in my after life." The priest's voice cracked as he whispered these words in my direction.

"You should be." I said and laughed wickedly as my fangs elongated and I spread my magnificent wings leaving the priest in a sobbing mess on the grass.

🌾🌾🌾🌾

As I soared higher in the sky; I breathed and transformed to the normal version of my vampiric bat-form; in case I needed to rescue humans. I knew I was still frightening but not as scary as full on demon vampire. I saw the mass of zombies attacking the entire town while the sirens went off. I touched down and slaughtered zombies trying to break into a home and eat the new family that had just moved here from New York. Then I saw a few ghoulish creatures of the night trying to attack the high school and I flew down and picked the three creatures; up and away from the poor Principal trying to stand up to the monsters.

"Thanks for saving our early weekend staff meeting Sheriff Midnight." The Principal and teachers from the windows of the school called out.

But as I looked back the other teachers did not look happy or thankful. *They all look absolutely miserable to be going into work on a*

Saturday. I thought and then couldn't help but wonder if I actually saved them or left them to their doom.

But in my worry I couldn't stop for day celebrations as it was now going on 8:00am and the whole town looked like a full blown battle zone. Buildings were exploding and screams could be heard throughout the streets. This was only the beginning of the war that would start in Trenton and consume the planet if not stopped. I quickly carried the ghoulish creatures far away from the people and killed them in my grip before disposing the beings into some open graves at the cemetery. *Snacks forever; this is the only good thing about the end of the world. I can stock up on body parts so I can make stews and soups.*

🌾🌾🌾

I flew higher as I scoped out the horror show of a town being overrun with zombies. The more I looked the worse it seemed to be getting as even nature seemed to be off. I watched as a large group of rabbits were eating what appeared to be the remnants of Farmer Magland. The vegetarian mammals were really ripping into the blue corpse and it was shocking for me to see even though I dreamt of eating the farmer many times. I was just going to intervene when another horror sight caught my attention.

I flew down heading straight for Grandad's. The local restaurant was crammed full of seniors eating breakfast and all had no idea there were vampire knights outside trying to sneak in through the back kitchen door. The knights were dressed in black armor and smelt like a thousand deaths and the swamps of hell. Then there were another massive group of zombies slowly on their way to the restaurant like the breakfast bell had been rung.

I raised my hand and said very loud the words which brought forth my armor and sword from the muddy cave wall; "Abracadabra." Suddenly I had on my full suit of armor that allowed my massive wings to be free and I carried Excalibur; bringing my sword of justice to fight the vampires with. I moved to the first vampire that immediately attacked. As I was fighting one off, the other two tried to attack my back. But I had been through many battles and these vampires were young knights that hadn't much training as I easily fought them off; and swung at the metal flag pole severing it. While it crashed down one vampire knight mockingly said; "Look at the great King of Avalon that can't even hit us. Some General you are Pendragon."

They all laughed at me only for one more second as I easily fended them off with my right hand and then I laughed back deep and hearty. The vampires were now looking at me with slightly worried expressions. But it all didn't Matter as in the next second I bent down and impaled all three with my left hand still gripping the flag pole. Their last gasps had come as I laughed even louder before they all caught on fire.

All these battles and the sun had not risen. The foreboding sky remained dark even though it should have been bright. It was an eerie morning of blood red skies and no warmth of the sun cursing me as I began to slice heads off zombies attacking the front door to the restaurant.

As soon as I was finished hundreds more zombies came out of the woods behind the baseball field across the street. As I charged forward I saw Julia and stopped suddenly.

"My Darling, you should be at home." I said tenderly as I placed my hand gently to her face and she immediately kissed it.

"My Love I can't find Jack anywhere. I am heading to the quarry to protect the teenagers as I suspect they might still be there from last night." Julia said as she stood on her tip toes to kiss me and closed her eyes.

I grabbed her in my arms and dipped her low in a romantic kiss. *You have my heart.* I said in my mind and she kissed me back much more passionately when hearing the words in her mind.

"Keep safe my sweetheart and grab Jack and then go home. This is only the first and second wave. There will be much gruesome creatures coming for me. I have to find the source and stop this rampage before the coming of the third wave or all is lost. Please be on the lookout for Oliver. I can't find him anywhere and I fear the worst my Love." I said gravely as she nodded with little tears; and gave me another kiss and hug.

In a flash Julia was gone and I returned to charging at the slow moving mass of zombies; severing zombie heads and green and blue blood oozing all over the field. Then I enjoyed impaling another group of vampire knights who were eager to fight. They had tried to rush me as I finished with the zombies but it was to their demise; as I was able to slice down another flag pole and move quickly impaling them all in one swift action.

The field looked like something out of a thriller movie as guts oozed out of headless bodies and then bursts of blue flames appeared in the vampires bodies attached to the pole stuck in the ground. Then a sea of ash blew through the field as the wind had picked up and purple lightening touched the ground. The earth shook as I started to worry even more about the fate of my two Sons. *It's happening all at once. I have to get my feelings under regulation. I am controlling the natural disturbances in the planet in my worry and anger.*

🌾🌾🌾

CHAPTER 31

JACK

He could hear the peaceful crickets around him and his tired eyes fluttered opened for a second as he got a shiver. His eyes caught the holographic shimmer of a wing under his arm and he hugged the person in front of him tighter as her soft hand squeezed him back. *Where am I again? Oh right, I remember I am being held captive by Ella. She is so strong. I am hugging her for warmth and protection from myself. And she is a fairy. And I think I am in love.* Jacks thoughts shifted as he listened to the soft snores of the girl of his dreams snuggled in his embrace. His nose was covered by her hair and he didn't care. The scent of the quarry roses was always intoxicating to him and that was exactly what her soft locks smelt like.

This morning was cooler and the thick purple fog surrounded him and his friends in some magic circle. He was too tired and too content by the person that now turned to face him while she slept. She placed her arm around his waist and he felt her warm breath on his chest now. There seemed to be fireflies twinkling around them. But the birds were absent this morning as he was forced to close his eyes; being suddenly stricken with an extreme happiness fatigue.

None of it mattered though. Not the mysterious purple fog. Not the poisoned toad tea. Not even the fact that he had been bested by a fae. All that mattered right now was that for the first time in his life he felt loved by the girl of his dreams. She had chosen him back and now he had a girlfriend.

His head ached and his eyelids remained closed while he listened to her steady heart beating to the similar rhythm of his. He smelt again the wild roses in her hair that forever more would make him think of her. He felt that honeyed breath of hers against his chest each time she snored and he smiled to himself. *Nope. Nothing else Matters except right here and right now.* The world could burn but he would relish in this moment of both of them being eighteen and in the arms of a sweet love.

🌾🌾🌾🌾

CHAPTER 32

LANCELOT

Lancelot was snickering at his ingenious plan and he put a deep sleep over anyone that might have been waking with his presence there. *Wow, I am so brilliant. Julia was a lot easier to get with those horse tranquilizer darts. I'm just going to put her in the protection circle with the teens. There is no way I'm sharing her with the zombies. After all, someone has to bear my glorious children after hell takes over the world.* Lancelot's thoughts were chipper as he gently laid Julia on the soft grass within the circle of magic purple fog.

He took one look at them all and then left stopping just outside the thick layer of fog which now had a six foot gapping space. He broke the barrier in placing Julia within the circle. And he knew what would happen if he left in haste; so he re-cast the protection spell.

He looked at his magnificent work of the completed circle of purple fog, once more. It wasn't just fog. This stuff was potent against any evil creatures. The purple fog would protect and kill any monster that dared to cross into the dense smoke. The bonus part of the spell was that it kept everyone inside of the circle, in a deep sleep now.

The spell would keep them all hidden from the world until he decided to break the spell or he died. But death wasn't an option. He was already of the undead variety. And if he passed from this body there wouldn't be any second chances. There wouldn't be any do-overs; his Boss would just keep his soul.

Lancelot thought about how invincible he raised his hands and summoned the hell hounds into the second wave attack on the town of Trenton. *First I will take this stinking town and then I will conquer the world. Everything is going exactly to my plan. Now I just have to capture one of the hopeless dark unicorns. I swear my wicked plan is like art with the eclipse happening for the next six hours. It's a masterpiece of evil and perfect timing for the end of the world. Even if Pendragon goes to full strength I can slay him. I am the destroyer of the world, not him. Hell better start promoting me or else I'm taking the throne after this.* Lancelot smiled wickedly at that last thought as he skipped past the grave in the forest singing the merriest of melodies under the bleeding sky of the eclipse.

🌿🌿🌿🌿

CHAPTER 33

MIDNIGHT

One vampire had gotten a good fist to my face as I spit blood on the ground and the acid from my mouth scorched the earth. So I shoved Excalibur so far up the lucky vampire's arse that instantly he burst into flames through the soft rain. I sighed as I watched some hell hounds race towards me and hundreds of zombies come for me and for the town.

This was the fight I had lived for. It was the fight I was exhumed from my grave for; but after the good knights had been burned by the Pope for saving the earth from evil it really left a bad taste in my mouth about who I was actually serving. I lived for conquering hell's armies but right now, my increasing worry left me distraught. Even in vanquishing the neverending enemy I still had no idea where my family was and if they were safe. I had been succeeding in slowly pushing the hordes of dark creatures back and defeating them before they had the chance to run wild through my beloved Trenton. But I had to work faster and find the source of the gate through the forest. If I didn't close the doorway to hell before the third wave, this battle would be even greater and the earth would be lost in horror and blood. The deadliest demons hadn't even been released. They would come after the war was won and collect the spoils of the victors. When the demons came to feast mankind would be doomed for a thousand years of darkness reigning supreme terror over the earth.

Right now, I wasn't winded but I was getting frustrated. The slaying and impaling was liken to folding the boy's laundry. Of all the times I folded it neatly for the lad and placed it perfect in the boy's dresser drawers; only to put more clothes in and be aghast by how messy everything was minutes later. That was exactly what this was like as I surveyed the land and started flapping my great wings faster and faster; making all of the sea of monsters blow back from the field into the forest.

Then I charged with Excalibur and continued to slay all the creatures coming for me as I thought about my family and if they were safe. I had to believe in the hope that Julia found Jack and Ollie. I made a prayer that I hoped would be heard as I slashed through zombies, vampires, and hell hounds. *Please Father, I know my soul is dark with tyranny. But I still serve thee and stand against the forces of evil with ye. Please guide Excalibur's blade to strike through the enemy and bless my eyes to find the hell gate and close it. And please assist me in not destroying the earth in doing so.*

Suddenly, my sword glowed with a blue holy flame as it sliced through the evil throughout the forest and I made ground in taking back my earth. Hours and hours passed of slaying thousands of evil creatures and then the forest was quiet with countless bodies of the fallen. *The second wave is finished I have to stop the third and final wave. I have to close the portal before the demons are unleashed and before I lose my temper. There is only one way. I have to stop the person responsible and use their blood to seal the portal.* As I flew through the forest I smelt the familiar scent of my human's blood outside another little cottage in the deepest part of the forest.

With such a thick scent of Ollie's blood; my claws and fangs elongated further uncontrollably as I sheathed my sword in breathing deeply the aroma of my friend's death. The bouquet was too thick, too heavy; as I busted through the roof of the cabin to find it empty. Immediately, I went to the table sniffing the blood and seeing it in a dried trail leading to a large crimson puddle on the floor.

My fury was too intense suddenly and I had to stop myself from transforming to the thing hell had created me to be. My hand had enlarged at seeing the sight and the smell; and it took all of my will to stop the change from coming. But I raged and roared so unholy that the cabin shook and the sound vibrated long and could be heard by every townsfolk and magic folk in hiding.

I smashed through the cabin's room smelling the disgusting scent of the lustful ogre and even more lust filled witches. I flipped the bed in anger at knowing what had happened by the dried trail of my human's blood. *Ollie suffered while two creatures were in here having deep relations. The smell of those disgusting monsters is as strong as Ollie's blood. One of them had deeper magic than the other though. I can smell the woman was in love but the male was wearing a mask. It was a very strong magical mask of deception; the male ogre had worn to trick the seer. That is the only way the portal could be opened with blood.* I went back to the kitchen table and clawed through the plasma. I rage roared again as I punched a wall breaking it through to find a hidden distillery of a moonshine operation labeled toad tea. Then I roared so high and violent that everything exploded in the room. That was the only thing that made me smile for one second as I discovered who these treacherous revolting creatures were. *If those witches are still alive they shall pray for death when I find them. Only one would need to be sacrificed on the altar. I now know where I have to go but I need to find my family.* I thought as I stormed out the cabin and waved my hand once and the cabin set to flames. I walked past the creepy scarecrow and burned it along with the garden.

⚜⚜⚜⚜

I continued on the path leading deeper into the woods. Everything was still. Then I came to a certain section of the river where a fresh grave was and a long manicured hand was desperately digging out of the dirt. *I got you.* I thought as I dug my claws into the green flesh and pulled the undead witch from the grave she was trying to claw out of. Then I quickly grabbed her throat as I held Excalibur to her chest that was missing her heart.

"Well now Hexia. I see someone has taken the time to raise you from the grave but left you damned and crawling on your belly to creep back to life. I'm feeling generous. You shall tell me where my Son is and I shall make your death quick." I ungentlemanly shouted in her face as I felt my fangs grow even larger.

"You can't kill me. I am back and your Son is long dead. I will never tell you a thing about the man I love; even if he did eat my heart and drown me." Hexia tried to get out as I gripped her neck tighter still holding her to my face so she could see the rage of fire in my eyes.

"You are wrong Hexia. He brought you back wrong. To be a vampire you still need a heart. He has disgraced you into being less. You are nothing more than a glorified zombie. He used you and now I know who he is. And your brains will give me the confirmation I need."

I shouted and then chopped off her head.

I hated all the co-conspirators in the toad tea moonshine operation; but I hated them even more now because they were involved. I was still determined to find my Son. But I needed to do something with Hexia's zombie body. I started ripping into her and took great pleasure in eating her brains to see her memories. I dropped to my knees at seeing Ollie dying on their wooden table and not one of them tried to save him.

I set the rest of Hexia on fire and snapped my fingers to the other dimension which her soul was sent to. It was a special place I constructed in hell where the truly evil ones were sent to be punished by my demon army. I stood before my demon vampire soldiers and the four captors that were in chains as the flames burnt their skin. The chains were around the necks and their feet and arms; and I snapped my fingers in making them fall to their knees.

"You shall spend all of eternity here. No kindness and no mercy shall ever find you. This is the last time you shall ever see each other as I will be separating you. Each of you will be tortured and then ate slowly; over and over in the flames where there is no salvation, no hope of redemption. The line you have crossed is permanently marked on each of your souls and it is too late for you. Merrideath, Hexia, Lucinda and Dufferin; you have been charged and are sentenced for all of eternity. This is in regards to the highest of treachery against The Oneness. The Father is of the purest love. And that is why he created the demons in fulfilling the punishment needed for the odious crimes which are committed. I damn you all now, for the torturing and killing of one of the Father's purest of creatures; and for your roles in starting Armageddon. You are forever cursed to the flaming pits of hell. Demon soldiers please take them away; I never want to see their putrid eyes again. And eat all of their tongues after you have recorded a few years' worth of their screams. I'd like to make a lullaby horror song to play to

warn any humans that survive this war; in hopes that it saves their souls."
I said and then raised my hand in burning their eyeballs out of their
sockets as they screamed and were dragged away by my loyal soldiers.

Then I snapped my fingers and returned back to this dimension and
to the forest. I quickly got back up from my knees with gritted fangs.
After severely wiping the blood from my eyes I went over and stomped
on the ashes of Hexia's body. I continued through the noiseless forest
with my eyes in flames as I could feel the heat of anger rising from them.

☘☘☘☘

Not one screeching vulture or leaf crunching rabbit could be heard.
They knew I was angry and they were not only in hiding from the evil
monsters loose but they were in hiding from my wrath. *If I see even one
cottontail right now; I swear I'm going to bite its face off and then suck
its brain and eyeballs right out of its fluffy skull. I'm so fuming; I could
drain the whole town right now.* My enraged thoughts were on fire as
my red eyes seemed to light the way in the darkness of the woods.

Even in making those devious creatures pay; it didn't bring me
satisfaction as I flew further into the dense woods determined to find my
Sons but not knowing what condition they were in. *I can't believe that
lying witch. I won't believe Oliver is gone. Hexia would say anything to
save her own skin; even in betraying her family to keep him satisfied. All
for what? The price of what she did; the price of what they all did; will
have no relief and no repayment of blood and screams will be too great
for their eternity spent.* I couldn't help the sharp pain in my gut at my
endless worry and those thoughts didn't give me pleasure. I felt like I
was going to vomit from the weight gnawing my undead heart.

I exhaled loudly as I watched the dark unicorns slowly moving
through a meadow. They had been the last of their kind and the Devil

had released them from their prisons. It must be because the darkness was winning and hopes and dreams were starting to die. The unicorns were no longer silver; their coats were mangy and the bones of each could be seen through their hanging skin. The group looked blackened from the soot's of the chimneys of hell. They were now damned creatures; empty shells of magic the demons had feasted and drained.

Then I stopped dead in my tracks as I saw one dark unicorn sent from hell carrying a body. It was unholy pregnant as it carried the lifeless human on its back. Its oil filled hooves still smoked from the fire pit that it had trotted out of and its skin was burning the flesh of the human that was hanging over its back.

"Noooooooo." I roared and flew down grabbing my Son and embracing him tight as we flew away from the field of loneliness and misery.

I clutched him to my chest but couldn't look at his face yet; as I felt the coolness in his blue skin. Very gently I flew downwards and softly touched the earth near some weeping willows.

"My boy. My sweet darling boy. Why did you get captured? God Why? I am so sorry, my sweet Son. My beautiful boy, I'm sorry. I should have been there for you. I should have told you, I adopted you from the moment I found you. I should have told you how much I loved you. Please, please say this is a dream and you are pretending. Please come back to me. Do not go to that light. Stay with me Son. I have so many truths of the universe to tell you and the secrets of life. My beautiful boy, come back to me." I held Ollie's lifeless body even tighter and rocked him back and forth as a sea of memories of feeding him soup and taking care of him through the years flashed through my mind.

As I was rocking with Ollie's breathless body my giant wings covered us both in protection. The forest was quiet except my pained sobs and the day seemed even darker with the crimson clouds thundering above the red and purple skies.

"I am so sorry my best friend. I am so sorry I couldn't save you. But I punished your killers. I couldn't be there for you but I will rain a terror of retribution on the other monster that helped do this to you." I cried as I hugged Ollie's corpse longer unable to stop the blood tears flowing steady out of my eyes.

"I love you my boy; my sweet little angel. Yes, be with The Oneness. Go far away from what I am going to do next. Be at peace my beautiful Son. I shall miss our breakfasts together and our long talks. I love you my Son forever and in my heart you shall stay." I said and I meant the words but I was lying to myself.

I wasn't ready to part with him. I couldn't let Oliver go. He couldn't leave to the Heavens. It was the one place I could only stand by the pearly gates and never be invited back in. If he stepped into the light he was gone from me forever. And so I did the only thing I could to keep him and sank my teeth into Ollie's neck.

I couldn't stop the tears as I drank the last of Ollie's dead thick blood and ruthlessly tore a chunk out of my wrist to let my flowing blood fall into his mouth and into the wound on his chest. Then I cried out into the darkness in sheer heartache at what I was doing. *I need more time with you my human Son. We still have a whole ocean of mermaids to kiss and release; maybe even eat. We still have many more memories to make my beautiful boy.*

As I made my wrist heal; I continued to rock and kiss Ollie's cheek. I hugged him even tighter for another moment before I set him down gently on the grass. I feverishly started digging a deep hole; much deeper than an average grave. I was digging faster and faster throwing mounds of dirt everywhere. Then very carefully I grabbed my sweet Oliver's body very delicately laying him down inside the hollow earth. But instead of leaving him I clutched him tight again with my wings wrapped around him. *Not like this. He is my son and deserves better than the bare earth.*

I closed my eyes and summoned my coat and the quilt off his bed Julia had made him. He needed to be warm for when he slept and I wrapped him in both. I rocked and hugged him for a few more minutes and then with tears streaming down my face; summoned my velvet lined casket and three chests full of magical healing soil from Wallachia and Avalon. I had brought them with me on my ship and they were the only thing that could bring someone back from the dead the right way as a new child of the night.

As the chests hovered; I held him tight and kissed his cheek once more. Then defeated but hopeful, I placed Oliver carefully in the casket and closed the lid. The sound seemed to echo off the trees as I couldn't stop the steady stream of blood falling on the casket and in the hole.

I slowly climbed out and emptied the rest of the magic soil all over the casket. My blood tears weren't stopping as I tried to continue to be strong but I had to halt. Suddenly I turned my head and puked as I had to cover over the casket were his sweet freckled face was lying inside.

Then I looked up to the heavenly sky of storm clouds swirling and placed my hands up in surrender. *Dear Oneness, please; I need my family. I need both my Sons. Ollie's life was taken unjustly and life has been so cruel to him. Let me bring him life everlasting as we serve you.* I got down on my hands and knees; begging for mercy and for The Oneness to hear my pleas and prayers. Then I stood up and took the last chest of dirt into my hands and physically buried my best friend and Son; completely.

I traced an ancient runic symbol meaning *'rebirth';* from the Celts and Welsh lands dated back to the vikings and the very first vampire. As I placed my hands out to the grave, I started singing an ancient Celtic lullaby; and immediately a wild rose bush started growing and blooming abundantly. The foliage was luscious cranberry and the roses were plush yellow representing the friendship that we had shared. I continued to sing as my tears continued to fall and the rose bush grew wild.

Then I stood there in silence, for a very long time as I wrapped my wings around me like a coat. I couldn't help but look to the roses in longing for what had been taken from me. I crouched down with both hands on the dirt and closed my eyes.

"I am sorry my Son. I can't do it. I cannot say goodbye my Beloved. I refuse. I love you too much. You will come back to me. It's not too late. You shall comeback and we shall be Kings together for all of eternity. We shall find you a castle and a bride. You will see it will be great. Gently sleep for a little while and then rise for me. When you awake I shall be here waiting for you my Dearest Oliver. Life was cruel but now it shall be everything you ever dreamed of; you'll see. I'm going to make all your dreams and wishes come true. And you shall be strong; no one will ever hurt you again. I can promise you this. We shall be a family once more. I love you. I love you my Son." I said as I gently patted the fresh earth sealing the drawn magic symbol and whispering magic words in another language.

Afterwards, I couldn't bear to leave. I just stood there lingering and looking on at the giant rose bush continually blooming as the cycles of life were restarting underneath. I could hear the thunder booming from up above but I didn't shrug off the heavy rain which seemed to be falling only on my heart.

🌾🌾🌾🌾

"My Darling what are you doing?" Julia shouted as she placed her hand on my shoulder and I shivered at the coldness in her strange touch.

I quickly wiped the blood tears from my eyes and face as I was speechless at what I had just done to escape the pain. I just looked at my beautiful wife and stood up to hug her as I sobbed.

"There, there honey. What is wrong? You have done such a good job at defeating the armies of hell. Are you tired now? I found the altar let us go quickly before the next wave starts." Julia said as she tried to move me but I was unmovable.

The wind picked up and I found myself downwind from Julia; and the scent of Oliver's blood and deception off her skin.

"Did you find Jackie boy? I need to know if he is safe." I said as I deeply inhaled my wife's hair and smelt brimstone instead of lavender and wild roses.

"Yes my Dear; he and the other teens are safe. They are in a protection circle. They have been unharmed and hidden in the quarry for their safety." Julia said as they started slowly walking away from the roses and started moving up the mountain.

"Were you trying to bring someone back? That symbol on the earth is forbidden. You know this Artorik."

"Who says it is forbidden?"

"He was already dead Pendragon can't you just let him go? I mean why does this kid mean anything to you? He is just more food for the demons which are coming unless we stop the next wave." Julia said very harshly and I stepped back smelling the magical mask scent from earlier.

"How did you know it was Oliver and that he is completely dead? I never mentioned Ollie's name." I asked as I placed my hand on Excalibur.

"It's because I was there silly. I was having fun while Oliver lay there dying. It's such a shame too. His sweet blood would've been a good year. Virgin twenty-three I believe; what a waste." Julia said as she violently transformed to Lancelot's vampiric form.

"It's you. You did this. Where are my wife and other Son?" I shouted as Lancelot laughed while he brought forth a black sword and slashed me.

"The great and powerful King Pendragon was crying like a giant baby bat. Who is this creature that is supposed to lead hell's great armies and destroy the world? Not the being before me. You are weak and so I killed Jack; and made love to your wife while she screamed my name over and over. Her neck was the softest I had ever touched as I accidently broke it while kissing her. But her blood was good. All of her juices were; especially the blood in her heart." Lancelot said and laughed again.

"Lancelot you are done for. You won't come back this time. Merlin told me, days before he passed away. He had seen your end in this moment." I shouted as I lunged with Excalibur but Lancelot moved.

Lancelot managed to do a quick hit into my side and my hand went to my bloodied side as I took a real good look at the black sword.

"Your wife tasted so good. Her pelvic bones were the best I ever crunched on. You should have eaten her while you had a chance." Lancelot laughed as he moved away from me.

"I know what you are doing and I have lived too long on this earth for such baiting. I know the oracle and I know what will happen if I lose my temper. I will not be transformed and used by hell any longer. I refuse to be the puppet to end the world." I shouted as I swung and missed Lancelot who seemed to be enjoying himself too much.

"You don't know shit Midnight. You don't know where you sent me the first time you killed me. I was devoured for all the flesh I had eaten in life. I was ripped over and over; and then even more painfully consumed in a longevity spell in the flames of the pit. It was an eternity that stretched on forever. You have no idea of anything. That was why I jumped at the chance to come back and kill you. I shall be the puppet and become the most powerful of creatures in destroying the earth.

Trenton is only the beginning, next will be the world. It will finally be me. I will be given my due right and become the last true King of Earth. And nothing will be left; I will scorch it to the core." Lancelot wickedly said and then laughed like a maniac.

I rolled my eyes. Lancelot couldn't defeat me then and wasn't going to defeat me this time. We were at a stalemate it seemed. No matter how many forms Lancelot took he would always be weaker. Suddenly, I started laughing louder than Lancelot; as I took another glance at something I just noticed. And Lancelot stood there with a puzzled look on his face.

"You laugh at me? But clearly I have overpowered you. Do you not see the blood still on this sword?" Lancelot took a swipe with his black sword but missed as I slashed his arm.

"Yes, you bear the Spear of Destiny. I can see the greatest of all weapons in your unworthy hands. The Luci-forge was the only thing re-built in hell to destroy Excalibur and it was forged from a great sin. But I know something you don't." I said and then laughed again and slashed Lancelot's other arm.

"What is that?"

"It is missing a huge piece of steel. It isn't whole. In breaking the weapon you have given me the advantage I need. I am invincible." I said very dark and grinned as I thrust my sword deep into Lancelot's chest and moved it down.

I was slowly gutting him like the garbage fish he was, exactly where he stood. Lancelot gasping fell to his knees dropping the Luci-forge.

"No, this wasn't how it was supposed to end. Now you will never know how I made both Jack and Ollie suffer. I made them watch me with Julia as I slit her throat and drank her. Then I killed them." Lancelot said out of breath but managed a pained smile.

"You lie even in death." Midnight said as he took Lancelot by the scuff of the front of his armor.

"You will never find where I hid their bodies. Because I ate them." Lancelot choked out those last words and tried to laugh before I became so infuriated I ripped out his throat.

"I am the only one who gets to win Lancelot. That is why I am the King and you will only ever be a servant of hell." I said and chuckled and then stopped as I saw three silk pieces of cloth fall from Lancelot's breast plate.

Three handkerchiefs had fallen to the ground all with the initials *A.P.* and embroidered with a crown. *Only the boys and Julia have those. Was Lancelot telling the truth? And now...I will never see them again. I will never see my boys or make love to my beautiful wife.* With those last thoughts my heart broke and I became enraged; chopping Lancelot's head off and setting his body on fire.

This was it. This is what set me over. I was pushed to the brink of devastation and started uncontrollably transforming immensely larger, and becoming the ultimate being of destruction. I was becoming the beast; the demonic dragon set to destroy the world. It was the doomsdays' prophesy in real life. This was the fate of the world with no hope for humanity as I was now lost in anger and hate; and I roared savagely in pain. My heart couldn't stop aching at what had happened to my family. *All is lost.*

I flew down the mountain and started breathing fire on the soccer field; eating any creature or any human in my path. The ash was so thick it filled the air making the storm even wilder as the winds picked up and darkened the already red sky past the boundaries of Trenton and over to the surrounding countryside's and sea-fairing communities. *Looks like I am the Bringer of Doom. I can feel my broken heart controlling the ocean tides right now. The pain is so great. I need to control myself but I can't. If I only had the bodies, I could say goodbye or bring them all back from death. Ollie had been dead for hours; and I'm not sure I could even save him from permanent death. All is lost without my family. Damn the earth and damn life. If I can't have my family no one can have happiness. From being a crusader for the forces of the light to now being the ultimate bringer of darkness and damnation; this has been a change but I can't stop the pain and need for vengeance. My heart hurts too much to consider a life without all of them. Death to all who confronts me now. All is lost. All is lost of me.* And with all those last thoughts I felt what little humanity left inside me; turn to brimstone and ash. I surrendered to my destiny and became what I was re-born to do.

I really was going to destroy the earth just like the prophesy and all religions around the world had predicted. *All is lost. The pain of sorrow is too great for me to bear alone. Death by flame to all.*

🌾🌾🌾🌾

CHAPTER 34

JACK

All of the teens awoke in the quarry and rubbed their heads as the pain seared through them. The growl had hurt them all and they clutched their ears to try to make it stop as they felt the pain of a beast that was roaring and bringing fury to the town.

"Oh my God, Mom we need to get down to the town. Dad thinks we are dead and now the prophesy is coming true." Jack said as he looked at his Mom wide eyed and she gasped as she noticed the ashes falling from the sky.

"If the prophesy is true then we need to find Excalibur and kill him to save the Earth." Ella said as she helped Jack up.

"We can't kill my Dad. There has to be some small piece of humanity left inside him. Once he sees us alive he will change back. We have to believe in love. I read in his sacred books that they believed that love was the only way to conquer the darkness in the end of the world."

Jack said as they all started running through the forest and seen other magical creatures with spears and weapons.

Then they saw one great fairy King with Excalibur and a great Ogre Warrior with a broken tar-oozing sword; all running towards the painful roars.

"We are uniting to go and fight the beast. This is the end of the world. The beast's emotions are setting off a chain reaction in the earth and if he is not stopped the super volcanoes around the planet will erupt from their dormant dream state and create such a global cataclysm nothing will be left. I have seen the ocean tides from the sea nymph's mind and giant tsunamis will start in a couple of hours if the *Bringer of Doom* cannot be stopped. Children you can go and hide but everything will be over in a couple of hours anyways. Either way, this is not your fight." The King of the Fae said as the entire fairy clans joined from the surrounding areas and from across the ocean.

All magical creatures combined their armies and they had congregated into three massive groups; all traveling towards the roaring and where a crimson sky was getting darker by the minute except the glow of flames and the powerful ruby eclipse. Their plan was simple; trying to stop the beast at any costs.

"I am not going into hiding. This is my earth too." Ella said as she joined the army. "I am sorry Jack. But if you are wrong we are all gone. It will be a merciful death, I promise you. I love you, but we need a world to live in and your Dad is hell-bent on destroying us all." Ella called back before she left.

"I'm sorry Jack. I have to check on Selena's human family and my own. Keep safe my brother." Mike said and ran with Selena into the crowds of creatures.

Julia grabbed Jacks hand as she looked into his broken hearted eyes.

"Even though they have Excalibur and the unholy Spear of Destiny;

I still believe we can reach him too. I know where he is going. I can still hear his thoughts. He is too much in anguish to hear ours but we have to keep trying to speak to his heart. That is how we can save him and everyone." Julia said as Jack followed her transforming into werewolves and running quickly to their home so they could grab special items.

Then they started running again to where the mob of creatures and armies of humans had cornered the dragon. Jack and Julia gasped as they seen him now transformed even stronger than he had ever been. And even with the armies against the great demon dragon he had become; the beast was stronger and fighting with an unholy fire and massive razorblade fangs and claws.

❦❦❦❦

The great blue-black demon dragon had six sets of black-tar filled wings and six sets of blood red eyes; and its body easily was the size of the whole football field in the open stadium. Its fangs and claws were much bigger than anything anyone on earth had ever encountered. It was something only written by seers and oracles regarding the end of days.

As Jack and Julia came down through the trees they crashed through the glass doors of the local hardware store where townsfolk were already looting. People were grabbing anything they could use as a weapon including gardening hoes and pick axes. The humans were fighting zombies off and fighting alongside a few rogue fairies.

Julia slashed open a grain sack with her claws and hide behind a shelf to get dressed; using it as a dress. Jack found some overalls and transformed slipping them on while his Mother attacked some zombies with the baseball bat she had found.

"Are you ready Son?" Julia said as Jack helped her finish some zombies off with a shovel.

"Yes Mom. We have to try." Jack said as he held up a small, blue item.

Julia looked at them with a glowing smile more radiant than before; and then she placed on her head her wedding veil and a few picked wild roses. She held a small picture in her hand as well. It was the last family picture of all of them smiling and laughing. It had been taken a couple of weekends before and Ollie was hugging Jack. When Jack saw the small photo from her satchel his tears swelled up.

"We don't even know what has happened to Ollie. But the worst had to have happened if Dad is this far gone." Jack said as he wiped his tears and then grabbed some more weapons to take out zombies.

🌾🌾🌾🌾

CHAPTER 35

JACK

They ran as fast as their legs could carry them in human form. Jack and Julia were shoeless as they ran into the fight of zombies. The zombies were now protecting the great blue-black, demon dragon as it roared ferociously and ate anything in its way; including any allied creatures of darkness. *Oh no. He may be more beast than Daddy now. We have to try though. We have to Mom. We have to save Dad.* Jack thought as he turned to his Mom who nodded as her eyes held a floodgate of tears at the magical creatures that were trying to stab the dragon's scaled flesh but nothing could penetrate its thick skin.

"I can't do this Jack. I have been in love with your Father since the first moment I seen him in the forest. The world had never known a great magic such as his before. He has the most unique and beautiful soul I have ever seen in any other magical creature except for when you were born. We have been together for almost two centuries. I'm sorry my Baby. I love your Father too much. I cannot watch them hurt him. I cannot watch them try to kill him. If he should perish I would be lost too." Julia said and ran away crying into the sea of the war.

"Mom, come back. That's why you are needed above all others. I need you." Jack shouted as he heard her crying in his thoughts before she vanished in the crowd.

There was a full out war between the sons of light and the sons of darkness blocking the path to the great beast roaring and eating anyone in front of it. Jack could see a sword on the ground beside a fallen fae warrior. As the silver sword glinted in the light; it ringed in a frequency only he could hear telling him to come pick it up. *Excalibur, what are you doing here?* The sword had heard his thoughts but the language was ancient and Jack could never understand the songs it sang. Only his Dad could ever speak with the sword and decipher the tune of love because his Dad was the chosen one ordained by God.

Jack hit the approaching zombies over the head and reached for the sword which felt hot to touch. He couldn't understand the song but Jack could feel the anger of the sword. The sword would not be used to kill the chosen one. *Love is the answer. I have to make a scene and get my Dad's attention.* Jack thought as he secured Excalibur to his back using one of his overall straps and then looked for some higher ground. All of the buildings had been built low except a few which were partially demolished.

Then Jack seen it; the rooftop of the hardware store was the answer he had been running away from. It was a flat roof and the beast was now backing up into the sturdy brick building. Jack started devising a plan that he prayed would work to get his Dad's humanity back. The closer he got the more he could hear the thoughts of hopelessness and that broke his spirit. But he was determined to win his Dad's heart back as he climbed the fire escape to the back of the building. The hardware store roof was in direct sight of the demon dragon if he could just use the outside speaker and mic set up. *I hope the mic isn't destroyed from the last employee rooftop party we had up here...Oh thank heavens, it works.* Jack thought as he flipped on the speakers that had an axe in the wall above them.

"Dad, it's me Jack. I'm alive. Dad, I love you. I'm over here. Look it's me Jack." Jack shouted as the great demon dragon turned its head and all six eyes.

Jack actually got a cold chill as he felt the great dragon looking into his soul judging its worth and he hoped he wasn't going to get punished for being born of darkness.

"You are just what my mind wants to see. You are a figure of my imagination. You aren't real." The deep dragon's voice actually hurt everyone's ears each time it growled out words.

Then a low snarl came from the beast and made the earth shake below. But the giant creature turned from Jack and let out another loud roar of sadness as it went back to eating zombies and any other magical creature in its path.

"It's me, Dad; stop being stupid. I'm alive and right here. Remember you didn't let me go to any grade eight dances? You felt it was unsafe because I was going through the full moon phase and I got really mad at you. Remember Dad, I chewed through your favorite slippers?" Jack shouted as the beast turned its six eyes back to him.

"I remember I loved those slippers. But I loved my boy more and now he is gone. My Son is gone. Stop torturing me with this heartache." The giant demon dragon roared and spit fire but Jack ducked and wasn't harmed.

"Dad I love you. It's me Jack. Let's stop this nonsense and go have breakfast. I'm hungry Dad; can't you make me some bacon? Please

Dad." Jack shouted over the battle noises below and just jumped out of the way missing the spiked tail that came crashing towards him.

"Let me be. The memories are too painful. All is lost." The demon dragon howled and then roared again.

Suddenly the great beast reached out and grabbed Jack before he could flee. Jack dropped the mic as he was being held in the giant demon dragon's claws. Jack was mortified that he wasn't being squished because what was going to happen to him was way worse. He watched the massive jaws opening and the great forked tongued coming out to touch Jack's face.

He felt sick as the clawed hand was moving closer to the row of razorblade fangs. Then he looked over and gasped at hearing his Mother; that was now on the roof with her veil down and singing. It was a very old Celtic lullaby that she had sung to Jack when he was a baby and she always sung it to his Dad when they would do dishes together.

Jack watched as the dragon immediately turned to the maiden on the roof with her golden hair down and the veil that was hiding her face was now up. *My Mom really is beautiful and he sees her now. He hears her. Her voice has triggered the memories of his heart.*

"Apparition be gone from here. I cannot bear to see her. I cannot let her see what I have become in her absence." The growl was low but much softer as tears flowed out of its six blood-red eyes.

"Then come back to me. I have loved you in all lifetimes and will love you in every lifetime. You are my eternity Artorik. Come home dear. Let us leave together now. Come home to me." Julia spoke so soft and endearing the words seemed to make flowers bloom and songbirds start singing.

"I do not know how. I am lost to evil now. All I can do is gift to you my undead heart all over again. I am yours for eternity my beautiful wife-spirit." The great dragon growled out each syllable and ripped its black-tarred heart out of its chest.

The beast placed the massive heart and Jack on the roof in front of Julia like it was building a wall to protect itself against her warfare. Jack was in awe of the effect his Mother had on the dragon.

"But I am here in the flesh my Darling. Touch my hand and you can feel my heart beat for you. Touch my heart and you will see I am real just as you are King Artorik Dracule Pendragon." Julia softly spoke over the mic as the great demon dragon wept and she stepped around the giant heart that was as big as a boulder.

"But you are nothing but a ghost of my fantasies." The demon dragon roared but looked more intensely at Julia.

Jack ran to get out of the way but passed the baby blue item to his Mom before hiding.

"What is that weapon you have formed against me? I know I could not trust my heart with a spirit that wants to torment me. If you are deceiving me spirit you shall pay." The beast said but didn't roar and the black smoke which had been forming disappeared from its jaws.

"You shall have to come to me to find out. Come here my Love. Let me hold you one last time." Julia softly said into the microphone and the war stopped as everyone now watched the interaction between the maiden and the dragon.

The growling ceased and then there was a great rumble as the magnificent demon dragon transformed back to a giant armored demon vampire bat. Still freakishly in size but its armor slowly retracted back to under its skin, as a hidden defense. The demon vampire slowly flew over and touched down its clawed feet gently on the rooftop in front of Julia. It moved in with the force of darkness and it still held the six eyes and six wings but was now scaled to the size of the new creature that still did not resemble Jack's Father. The creature slowly walked past the giant heart that was slighter smaller than its new form.

Jack and Julia started crying as the creature came over and fell down to its knees in front of Julia. Julia rushed over and put her arms around the creature that still held an echoing of the former King. In the glint of all its onyx eyes there was something tortured left inside.

"You have to slay me with Excalibur. I am tired. I need to be set free from the demons trying to break through my soul. Restore the balance in my soul and the Universe. You have to kill me." The great demon vampire spoke deep and full of pain.

"I can't my Love. What if you don't come back? I need you. I could not live in a world without you." Julia said as she cried.

"You must my Darling. An act of true love is what I need right now and it is only with love that you can end my suffering. Please kill me, my Darling."

Jack cried as he heard the words the creature said but it wasn't his Dad's voice. This being held certain memories of the pain; but it was pure darkness and evil was consuming its soul from the inside. Soon there would be nothing left.

Jack walked over and hugged the creature too; that kissed the top of his head. Jack watched as Julia grabbed Excalibur and raised the sword but stopped just above the giant man-sized heart. Her tears flowed as they both looked at the new being that had blood tears rolling down its blue-black cheeks. The creature nodded as it looked over to Julia.

"Come home my King. I love you and we will wait for you for all of eternity. Come home to your family." Julia softly said as she stabbed the heart and it slowly turned to stone.

Jack watched as the creature seemed to start slowly turning to stone too.

"Dad this was what I gave Mom. It's my blue baby-booties that you knitted me and here is a picture of our family laughing and having fun. Remember us and come home Dad. I love you Dad. You will always be my hero." Jack hugged the creature tighter.

"I love you now and forever my beautiful Husband. My heart will always be yours." Julia said and joined in hugging her family.

"Thank you for saving me. I love you my fam..." The creature said just before it turned to stone completely.

The sun's rays of light shone down like a beam on the rock statue and the giant stone heart with Excalibur's handle sticking out. All the clouds disappeared and the weather became a beautiful sun filled day with cheers coming from down below the rooftop.

Everyone was celebrating; humans and magic creatures because the last of the dark horde was being pushed back into the mountain and Lancelot's blood was sealing the door shut with the fae army looking on.

While everyone was cheering and immediately drinking ale and mead; the rooftop still held its own gloom. Jack and Julia were still clinging to the statue while tears came down their faces. Then a soft breeze blew through them and in one more moment the creature that had vaguely resembled Jack's Dad crumbled away like he was only dust to begin with. It was like some cruel twist of fate as the gentle wind took the dust away and the once great King with it. Meanwhile no one knew the heartache on the rooftop of the family that had just lost their leader. As the celebration continued while the sun set; Jack started crying like a baby as he went and hugged his Mom.

"Mom, this isn't how it ends. It can't be." Jack sobbed as he cried in her arms.

"Don't give up hope Jack. Not all is lost. His heart is with us." Julia said as she looked over to the stone heart with Excalibur brilliantly singing to her.

🌿🌿🌿

It was the first time that magical creatures were exposed to the humans. The hidden realms were no longer secret; the end of the world had changed and evolved the entire communities' perception. Jack wondered how long it would last until the witches' supreme council would fly on their broom sticks combining *a natural disaster spell* with *a forgetting magical creatures spell.*

There was no way the magic world would let this co-existence stay because of the power struggle it always would come down to. *It's too bad this can't last; I love how open the humans are with the werewolves and other magical creatures.* Jack thought as he watched a flower fairy cheers an old man.

As he walked unabashedly as a werewolf; very quickly he carried the draped crater on his back. It was the only thing that mattered to him; next to his Mom who assisted him with doors. They moved swiftly in between party-goers; making their way through the happy mob dancing in the streets as the cheerful music played. Jack watched as Ella walked over quickly to him but he didn't stop.

"Jack I'm sorry. Can you please forgive me?" Ella said as she gently touched his arm.

"It's okay Ella. I know you were just doing what you had to. But I love my Dad. I hope one day you can see the great man he is and not the monster." Jack said as he kissed her tear-streaked cheek but continued to move carrying the extra-large covered item strapped to his back using a whole bunch of speaker wire.

Jack took his moment to leave just as her gaze broke from his, when some loud fireworks went off in the twilight. He was too far away and hidden in the crowd when he looked back to see her looking for him and calling his name.

Jack and Julia were headed up to a very special cave in the mountain. They looked down to the valley below and watched the purple moon dust across the sky through the fireworks. *The fireworks are a perfect cover up. If Dad was here right now he wouldn't need a potion he could just use his magic.* Jack thought as his Mother nodded in agreement but then she added to his thoughts. *Son, he is still here with us.*

As the evening of celebrations continued the supreme council went about sprinkling purple moon dust across the skies above the fireworks so it would fall over the houses and cottages of the fair town of Trenton and all the surrounding communities of Quinte West.

"Place the giant heart gently in the hole I dug while I start covering it with a layer of soil from Wallachia and Avalon; from a couple of the treasure chests. Then we wait." Julia said as she transformed to her wolf-form and frantically buried the giant heart with the sword still sticking out.

Just as she finished burying the giant heart a large cracking sound could be heard as Jack gasped seeing a male's hand come up from below. Julia then started digging frantically and stopped as they heard his familiar loud intake of breath that his lungs didn't need.

"My Love you saved me and the world. I knew you wouldn't give up on me." The deep voice came from his Dad that climbed out of the grave and Jack's jaw dropped.

Julia quickly transformed and wrapped them both in the canvas cover. Jack ran over and they stood there hugging each other.

"My Dear, Jack was the true hero; I couldn't bear to watch them attacking you. He was the one that tried to get your attention and then I came to both your rescue. I just didn't know how we were going to get you back until Excalibur sang to me." Julia said as she cried and kissed Midnight's regal face.

"You are both my hero's. You both always have my heart. Now let's leave the cave; I'm positive I need a long bubble bath." Midnight deeply said as his red eyes shed a few blood tears of happiness.

Jack rolled his eyes but laughed as his Mom giggled. His Dad reached over and wiped a few tears from Jack's eyes. *I'm so glad your back Dad.* Jack thought as he gave his Dad a big bear hug.

"Son, I am too ancient to die again completely. In fact, I am beyond death now. What you guys have done is set me free from the curse of the prophesy." Midnight said and chuckled.

"So your life purpose is fulfilled now?" Jack asked.

"My life purpose was fulfilled the day I found your Mother; and the day she home delivered a little bundle of my evil spawn of six pounds thirteen ounces; and it was fulfilled when we adopted an orphaned thirteen year old that was living under a bench in the winter. Family has always been most important to me. I was reborn to destroy the world but I was never about destroying the world. The Oneness created me with free will; even being born of darkness I choose to still walk in the light. We are all a part of the great plan of the Universe. Merlin believed in this too. The dragon inside will always be there but now you know how to slay the beast and get me back from the brinks of hell on earth." Midnight said and chuckled again as he fake-breathed deeply the scents of lavender and meadow flowers.

"Dad, why do you breathe like that? We all know you don't need air to function." Jack said and laughed.

"You see my evil spawn; sometimes you create such a habit of involuntary motions that even in death you can't stop. It's addictive trying to pretend to be human and live like the humans. For example; I could give up my royal birthright and my castle; but I could never live in this cold, dirty cave forever. Do you know what I mean Son?" Midnight said and his red eyes glowed when he smiled.

"I get it Dad; I wouldn't want to live in this cave either. I love our Egyptian cotton sheets too much." Jack said and everyone laughed as they transformed into wolves and ran through the forest to go home.

🌾🌾🌾

CHAPTER 36

MIDNIGHT

The weekend had been pretty hectic but now Monday morning was here. I smiled wickedly as I flashed my lights to chase down the bus and pull those teenagers over. One student in particular was in direct violation of code 666. My glasses remained motionless as I stood tall with my arms crossed on the hood of my patrol truck that was racing to catch up with the bus. My silver star danced a light on the back of the bus and my fanged smile seemed to grow the closer I got to the vehicle I was chasing down.

I sounded the sirens and the bus finally pulled over. No one was physically driving my actual patrol truck and the bus driver and students knew this. It was a typical Monday of giggles, horrified expressions; and a terrified driver that was watching me from the bus rearview mirror.

I didn't hide the fact I was floating past the long bus windows of wide-eyes and big-smiles. I kept floating to the front of the bus as everyone watched me stop and knock on the door. My glasses were on but my fangs were visible as I smiled quite creepy towards the shaken driver and the door still creaked open.

"Frank you know I need an invitation. Don't make this harder than it has to be. I'm still hungry from working the graveyard shift." I said in the deepest voice I could get away with; without making the human pee himself.

"Would you come in Demon Midnight? I mean, Sheriff Pendragon it would be an honor to have you on my bus. Please come in." Frank the bus driver said in a hushed tone that was equally as shaky as his hands cranked open the door.

Then Frank went back to white knuckling the steering wheel and facing forward without looking at me.

"Why thank you Frank. That is mighty kind of you." I said and chuckled as I floated up the steps and stopped in the aisle.

I looked at my smiling Son that had a blush across his cheeks but was still happy to see me.

"Jack you forgot your lunch and lunchtime is a very important meal of the day. Let this be a little lesson to you kids. I will hunt you down if you don't eat a good lunch every day. I want everyone to promise me this or else." I said in my even deeper voice and smelt a faint urine smell.

"Yes Sir, Sheriff Pendragon." All the teens said together as everyone watched Jack step forward and grab his paper lunch bag from me.

"Mister, I need a hug." I said as I grinned and the kids watched my fangs elongate.

"Thanks Dad, I love you." Jack said and gave me the biggest bear hug in the world.

"I love you too Son. See you tonight." I said and then floated back down the aisle and stopped right beside the bus driver.

"Thank you Frank. Have a good day, maybe I'll stop by for a bite later if you're free after the sun sets?" I said darkly and grinned again.

"I might have to let you know about that. I am feeling suddenly ill." Frank said gravely as he was sweating profusely.

"Oh, that's too bad. I was thinking we could have barbeque; I have this great little recipe. It'll melt the flesh right off the bone; it's that sweet and tangy." I said as I gave a chef's kiss and then turned to float down the stairs and past the length of the bus with my arms crossed.

"Carry on Frank. These kids need to get to school already." I said as I knocked on the bus three times and the engine roared to life.

The bus sped away as I listened to the teens chatting about being frightened and amazed at the same time. Some of the cheerleaders thought I was dreamy which made me smile.

Everything was back to normal. All the teens thought I was a demon and were still terrified of me. That was a good thing of course because it meant I could count on the rumors to continue and the teens to not push their luck too much. Everything was back to normal except I now knew about the secret rendezvous meetings between Jack and Ella at the quarry. *My Son has a girlfriend.* I thought as I heard Jack's thoughts before the bus disappeared completely down the road. *I love you Dad.*

⚜⚜⚜

Everything was back the same except one thing but I had been visiting the special grave in the woods. I had been carefully exhuming his body for the last six nights and giving him more of my blood. It had taken more time and he needed extra care but I could see him healing to his new vampire form. Just as carefully, I reburied him with the healing soil from Wallachia and Avalon. And I continued singing and talking to him as the rosebush grew and bloomed during the witching hour. His thoughts were timid to speak with me at first but were becoming stronger as he healed.

Tonight I was positive my family would be complete again. Once the moon was full of blood and high in the sky; I would be ready with the shovel and open arms. *What a wonderful Father's Day present to myself. I will have everyone together again. Who would've thought life could be this good after death?* I thought as I sped down the road and I looked over to see Merlin smiling at me sitting in the passenger seat.

🌾🌾🌾

♠The End♠

ACKNOWLEDGMENTS

I would really like to express my sincere gratitude to; The Universe, my fans, family, and friends. Its fine people like you that give struggling authors a chance. Thank you again!

I would also like to thank my mechanics and my friends Eric Heldman and Jay Flowers at Good Year Obsentia, in Quinte West, Ontario. Thank you for always being great friends and taking care of my car. I am so appreciative that you are lights in the world and practice random acts of kindness every day. Thank you again for not suing me for killing off your characters in future novels! Their website is here if you want some kind individuals helping you with your auto needs and are in the Quinte West Area: https://www.trentontire.ca/

Thank you for reading! I really hope you have liked my book. Please add a short review and let me know what you thought!

And always let your light shine bright!

ABOUT THE AUTHOR

A.L. Secord is a pen name for the author APRIL SECORD. She enjoys many genres. But she is most passionate about Dark Fantasy Romance. She loves learning new things, and occasionally burning food for the ones she loves. She is an author, a proud mother, and an avid adventurer of the unknown; on her many pursuits for greater happiness and Bigfoot.

Enjoy other books by A.L. SECORD

Check out other books written by this Author.

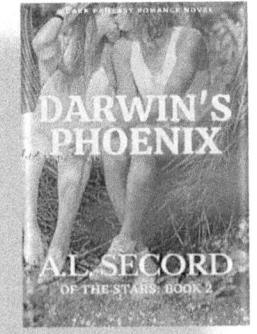

www.ingramcontent.com/pod-product-compliance
Lightning Source LLC
Chambersburg PA
CBHW070922180626
46817CB00003B/1173